"**FOUR STARS**:...The original Tinkerbell never had it so good... Steamy, sweaty sex abounds... After reading this, I will always think of Captain Hook as a hero, and Never Neverland will not be the same." --*Just Erotic Romance Reviews*

"**5 BLUE RIBBONS**:... Mardi Ballou writes a passionate and sensual tale... The amazing chemistry between the characters, combined with the intriguing storyline, made for a very hot and arousing read...
an exciting and erotic tale that is sure to entertain the reader until the very end." --*Romance Junkies*

"Hook, Wine & Tinker is a sexy, fast-paced romp... a well-written, fun yet deliciously sexy story that is sure to entertain."
--*Sensual Romance Reviews*

"...an erotic and enjoyable read. It features a sexy yet sensitive hero and a sympathetic heroine who faces a difficult choice. She must decide overnight in which man to put her heart and her trust: the Lost Boy or the Pirate." --*Romantic Times*

"The pages of this enchanting story sizzle throughout the book, and the heat level is set on burning... I was kept on the edge of my seat wondering what game this creative couple would play next... If you like your characters intelligent, thoughtful and possessing quick-witted humor, then be sure to read *Hook, Wine & Tinker* very soon. Ms. Ballou's next book is Pete's story and I can not wait!" --*eCataRomance Reviews*

Discover for yourself why readers can't get enough of the multiple award-winning publisher Ellora's Cave. Whether you prefer e-books or paperbacks, be sure to visit EC on the web at www.ellorascave.com for an erotic reading experience that will leave you breathless.

www.ellorascave.com

HOOK, WINE & TINKER
An Ellora's Cave Publication, July 2004

Ellora's Cave Publishing, Inc.
PO Box 787
Hudson, OH 44236-0787

ISBN #1-84360-890-1

ISBN MS Reader (LIT) ISBN # 1-84360-890-1
Other available formats (no ISBNs are assigned):
Adobe (PDF), Rocketbook (RB), Mobipocket (PRC) & HTML

Hook, Wine & Tinker © 2004 Mardi Ballou

ALL RIGHTS RESERVED. This book may not be reproduced in whole or in part without permission.

This book is a work of fiction and any resemblance to persons, living or dead, or places, events or locales is purely coincidental. They are productions of the authors' imagination and used fictitiously.

Edited by *Raelene Gorlinsky*
Cover art by *Darrell King*

# PANTASIA 1:

# HOOK, WINE & TINKER

Mardi Ballou

## Chapter One

Gwyn Verde bustled around the kitchen, getting her tiny cottage ready for what she fully intended to be a very special night with her boyfriend, Pete Payne. Superb food and even more superb lovemaking. And finally, last but not least, *romance*, the crucial third leg of the triangle. Pete did great with eating…food. As for their lovemaking… what it lacked in quality it made up for in quantity. But starting tonight, she was going to shoot for quality too. Which meant adding the romance. All the essential ingredients combined and intertwined, just like in her cooking.

She stirred wine into the already simmering tomato sauce, added basil, thyme, oregano, and enough garlic to sink Dracula. She sniffed appreciatively, anticipating how great the sauce would be on the handmade pasta, fresh from the gourmet shop's refrigerator. On her way home from her job at a travel agency, she'd picked up a Chianti that blew her wine budget for the month and a tiramisu guaranteed by the baker to make the tongue "weep with joy".

Gwyn's two settings of Lenox china, antique sterling, and Waterford goblets now graced the small, round dining table, covered tonight with cream damask and matching napkins. Cream colored tapers in sterling holders stood on either side of a bouquet of red and white roses. She'd rearranged each piece several hundred times until she was totally satisfied. Heck, her house gleamed and smelled like a romantic wet dream.

Looking at the clock, Gwyn realized she'd better hustle to be ready when Pete arrived. To stay relaxed, she thought longingly about the exotic interlude to the Fantasia Resort in Bali she'd packaged for one lucky couple's romantic getaway just that afternoon.

Romantic getaway. Weren't those among the sweetest words in the English language? She wanted to be headed off for a romantic getaway—with Pete, of course. Lots of places would do. But she dreamed of going to one of the Fantasia Resorts—billed as the places where fantasies and more were guaranteed. Naturally, fantasy fulfillment wouldn't come cheap, even with her travel agent discount. On the other hand, she and Pete together could swing a few days in lovers' paradise. After all, Pete was a computer programmer for the company that owned Fantasia Resorts. He'd probably be able to get an even better deal than she could.

Everything about Fantasia Resorts breathed romance. She could just picture herself there with Pete, who had a lot going for him, if only... At six foot with a slim build, sandy brown hair, and azure blue eyes, he could have modeled or maybe even taken a shot at Hollywood. But Pete was oblivious to his good looks—which had its pluses and minuses.

Unfortunately, Pete was oblivious to a lot besides what a hunk he was. While Gwyn was twenty-eight going on twenty-nine, Pete was thirty going on seventeen. Which was great in the bedroom, where he had the stamina and perpetual horniness of a randy teenager—but, alas, a teenager's total lack of sensitivity and awareness. "Slam bam thank you ma'am" had distinct limits she hadn't been able to cure him of—yet. She wanted more, both in the bedroom and outside it. Pete brought to life the old adage: "You can't have it all." Being a realist, she was willing to compromise. Just not about having romance in her life. Not any longer.

With dinner in progress, Gwyn moved to the bedroom. Black silk sheets, fat red roses perfuming the air, a mellow saxophone crooning love songs in a continuous loop on her CD player. That was as good as it was going to get. Now it was time to work on herself. She soaked in rose and jasmine-scented bubbles. Then she emerged from the tub, rubbed musk-scented cream from head to toe, and applied Pete's favorite perfume, vanilla extract, to all the strategic spots—behind her knees and ears, inside her wrists, between her breasts, and in the sensitive folds between her thighs and her waiting core.

She slipped into her brand new killer black dress and studied herself in the mirror. The dress hugged her curves, clinging to her perfumed breasts in a way that said, Touch me, Sniff me, Fuck me, Love me. At five foot two, she loved how tall she felt in her high strappy sandals. She twisted her long blond hair up, clipping one of the fresh red roses over her right ear. Full makeup to emphasize her green eyes and shapely lips. She smiled. She cooked like Julia Child and looked like a short Uma Thurman. Okay, slight exaggeration on both counts. But she looked and cooked pretty darn good—and better than ever tonight.

She was way ready for Pete. But was he ready for her? She looked at the clock, and began to pace.

A half hour late, he rang the bell. Gwyn bit back her annoyance. After all, Pete was chronically late. She knew that. She could live with that, if he'd just start meeting her other needs.

Pete stood in the doorway, grinning and holding up two plastic garment bags. Gwyn's heart began to race. Maybe he had some sort of romantic surprise in mind. She loved surprises.

"Hey, baby, am I ever glad to see you!" he exclaimed, racing in, dropping the garment bags onto Gwyn's black leather couch, and grabbing her into a clinch.

Feeling his erection pressed against her, Gwyn murmured, "I guess you are." She rubbed herself against him, savoring the promise of his hard cock.

He broke away from her, following his nose to the kitchen. He pointed to the simmering sauce and said, "Let's hold dinner." He looked her up and down. "First things first."

Knowing how much Pete loved food, Gwyn took his desire as a positive sign. Heck, the sauce could sit. Would probably taste even better. She'd just need to boil the pasta for a few minutes. And she could do that after...

Pete was nuzzling her, nibbling her neck, connecting with her in all her most sensitive spots. "Mmm," he said. "You smell real good—like warm cookies just out of the oven."

"You can smell me over the sauce?" Gwyn asked, surprised and pleased that he was paying such careful attention.

He waggled an eyebrow. "Hey, when Mr. Battery is ready to go, all the senses race into high gear."

"Mr. Battery?" Gwyn asked, wondering if Pete was somehow referring to her vibrator. They'd had a few brief conversations about gadgets and their uses, but Pete hadn't seemed real eager to include her vibrator in their lovemaking.

And he wasn't now. He pointed downward to his burgeoning erection. "Yeah, you know. Ever Ready." He chuckled.

She looked where he pointed and admired the visual. He was always giving his penis new names, some more interesting than others. No matter what he called it, the man had an available hard-on on demand.

Gwyn turned off the burner, and Pete led the way into her bedroom. She paused in the doorway, waiting to see if his newly heightened senses responded to the seductive scene she'd set.

Nope. "Hey baby, let's get naked," he yelled, rapidly discarding his clothes in random piles.

A flash of disappointment riffled through Gwyn. Lowering her voice to its huskiest, most seductive pitch, she said, "Pete, I'm wearing a really special dress. And trust me, what's under it is even more special." She licked her lips. "Why don't you undress me?"

Pete was already lying naked on her silk sheets, his erection rising like a periscope from his sea of wiry pubic hair. He sat up and looked at her, grinning. "Oh, baby you know I always fumble with the doodads. Heck, with you looking all gorgeous like that, I'd probably tear something. Get out of those duds and come here."

Okay. On to Plan B. "Pete," she purred, "watch me while I strip." She went into prime bump and grind mode.

Pete said, "Hurry. Mr. Battery's ready to pop."

Having experienced how rapidly Mr. Battery could pop, she quickly but carefully took off her sandals, dress, the sexy teddy, the lacy garter belt, the silk stockings with the perfect seams up the back, and her black thong, and stacked them on the dresser.

He was still half sitting up, watching her, his cock in hand. "Come here, baby," he called. "I've been waiting for you all day." He lay down when he saw her approach.

With a sigh, she stretched out next to him. As he kissed her, she let go of some of her frustration. She'd wanted a seduction scene. So it had taken all of three seconds for him to be seduced. She had to realize change took time. Mmm, that felt so good, what he was doing with his tongue, licking his way down from her mouth to that valley between her breasts, where he lingered for several seconds.

He groaned. "Oh baby, I can't take any more. I gotta come into you."

He wedged his thigh between her legs. At his touch, Gwyn felt herself begin to grow wet. "That's it, baby," he said, as he rubbed his thigh into her moisture. "Oh, yeah, you're so hot."

She arched her hips upward so her waiting folds rubbed against his thigh. Umm, yes. He was just at the right angle to get her clit. She rubbed harder and felt the beginning of a fast flash orgasm. Pete pulled away, and Gwyn reluctantly put her climax on hold.

Pete bit the top edge off a foil packet, pulled out the condom, and stretched it over his throbbing cock. "Ready, babe?"

Gwyn stifled a sarcastic comment about her abandoned come, opened her legs, and wrapped them around his slim hips. She gasped as he thrust into her even more quickly than usual, then began to savor the feel of him in her. Oh, yeah. She could tell he'd been waiting for this. Well so had she. "Pete, slow things down a bit."

He grunted a protest but managed to ease up a bit. Oh, that was so much better. He had this way of moving his hips so his cock touched every sensitive surface in her hungry core. She clutched his ass tighter to maximize her contact with his thick cock and nearly shrieked with pleasure when he began to tongue her ears, to bite her lips. She was really getting into it now.

And then he spasmed, and she knew he was going to come. She sped up her own rhythm to try to catch up with him. She was climbing up that mountain, the swirling sensations taking her up to that peak... He grunted again, released a small torrent, and collapsed on top of her.

Gwyn gritted her teeth. She'd almost been there. Again. She got caught mid-slope and was left hanging. Again. "Pete," she called out hoarsely. He rose, grinned, and rolled off her, careful to keep the condom secure around his still half-stiff mast.

"Pete," she called again. Her clit was throbbing, in search of a release that suddenly was receding further and further from possibility. "Pete, I need..."

He looked at her, his smile broad with satisfaction. "That was great, Gwyn." He stretched. "Let's go have some chow, then more sack time."

"Pete," she whimpered, "I'm not quite *there* yet. I need more from you. Now."

But he was already out of bed and throwing on his clothes. "I'm starving," he said, stomping out to the kitchen. "Feed me, woman. Then we'll play some more."

Gwyn strongly considered getting the real Mr. Battery out and giving herself what she needed. Would Pete even care?

After several moments of internal debate, Gwyn decided she'd cut Pete a break, go on with dinner. This wasn't the first time she'd ever put up with some frustration, and realistically she knew it wouldn't be the last. But this time, they had the whole evening ahead of them to banish her immediate frustration. Lots of opportunities to come. Literally. Now that he'd gotten his edge off, he'd surely be more responsive to her needs.

Now that they'd been to bed together, it felt kind of stupid to put on the killer dress and elaborate underpinnings again. Instead, she took out a pair of bikinis, decided to forego a bra, and threw on some jeans and a T-shirt. More reasonable outfit for cooking anyway.

Pete was already in the kitchen, guzzling her expensive Chianti. "That's supposed to be for dinner," she protested. "And you're just supposed to sip."

He shrugged and parked himself near the stove. "So, we almost ready to eat?"

"Hey, Pete, lots of opportunities here to help." Not that there was a lot left to finish, but it would be nice if he'd do more than stand there, watch her, and drink wine.

He made a face and continued standing in exactly the same spot. "Come on," he said. "I had a tough day. Besides, I get off on watching you cook."

She stifled her impulse to fling the wooden spoon she was stirring the sauce with at him. But Rome wasn't built in a day. And she'd rather concentrate on building his skills for romance than as a cook. Once she had the sauce simmering again, she set the water boiling for the pasta. She got the salads and breadsticks out, put the pasta on, and made a final check.

They were soon seated across from each other. Pete poured them each some of the remaining wine. "To us," Gwyn toasted.

"To Halloween parties," Pete responded, clinking glasses with her.

"Halloween parties?" Gwyn put down her goblet.

Pete swallowed his wine. "Yeah. That's why I brought the stuff over," he said, pointing to the garment bags Gwyn had temporarily forgotten about.

"What about Halloween parties?" she asked. Usually when Pete talked about parties of any kind, they involved giant TV screens and the Super Bowl or the World Series.

Pete inhaled some pasta. "Wow! This is great!"

Gwyn nodded modestly. "Thanks. So what is this about a Halloween party?"

He finished chewing and said, "My boss is throwing a party on his huge yacht tomorrow night."

"Your boss? On his yacht?"

"Yeah. It's docked here in San Diego."

She frowned. "Your boss, Joe Schmendrick, has a yacht?" Gwyn had met the mousy little guy once at a picnic. She'd pictured him more as the rubber ducky in the tub type than someone who'd own a yacht.

Pete shook his head. "Not my supervisor. The big BIG boss. Dominic Laredo. The guy who came up with the Fantasia Resorts concept and owns everything. He sails around all the time. Comes to land to collect his money and check out what the little folk are doing. This is the first time he's docked here in San Diego in months. We've set some new sales records for the resorts and this is his way of thanking us, along with raises, of course. He wants all his employees from the local office to come to his party — in costume. He'll have big prizes for the ones he likes best."

"Sounds like an overgrown kid," Gwyn muttered. She took a sip of her wine. She found something ridiculous about supposed adults putting on costumes and hanging out at a party no one over thirteen belonged at. On a deeper level, she found something delicious and possibly dangerous about people choosing to masquerade as other people. She wasn't sure how she felt about being in that kind of mode with Pete. "Do you have to go?"

Pete stopped chewing. "We," he said. "I really *want* to go. Should be fun. Anyway, we *have* to go. When Dominic Laredo says 'come to my party', people who want to keep working for him don't stay away."

"In other words, it's a command performance. Okay. So aside from forcing people to come to his parties, what else do you know about this Laredo guy?"

Pete shook his head. "Just what everybody else except you knows. Eccentric young billionaire and all that. I'm sure you've read about him in all those magazines you're always looking at. Gwyn, you'll love the party. I got us great costumes."

Right. The garment bags. What could Pete possibly have come up with for them? Romeo and Juliet? Lancelot and Guinevere? Maybe this would be the way to see if any romance lurked in his heart. "All right. I'll bite," she said.

"Wait 'til we get to bed for that," he leered.

She rolled her eyes.

"So you want to see the costumes?"

"I can hardly wait." Gwyn coaxed a bit more wine from the bottle into her glass. Pete didn't seem put off by her sarcasm. He jumped up and grabbed the plastic bags, opening the first to indicate green nylon tights, a tunic in a slightly darker green, and cap with a feather. Gwyn's heart sank. Neither Romeo nor Lancelot.

"You're going as the Jolly Green Giant?" she asked. What was she going to be? Frozen lima beans?

He laughed. "Good one, Gwyn. But you're joking, right?"

She didn't want to appear dim, but that really was what she thought of.

"I'm going to be Peter Pan," he said.

*Oh great*, she thought. *The quintessential lost boy.* That fit.

"And you," he said, lifting the other plastic cover, "are going to be Tinkerbell."

*Groovy. Just what she needed. To traipse around some spoiled rich guy's boat dressed like a flitting fairy.*

"I don't think so," she said, looking at the tiny pink costume made of a cheap, clingy polyester. No bra under that one. Pink iridescent wings fluttered as Pete moved the costume around.

He pouted. "Come on, Gwyn. Be a good sport. You know Peter Pan is my favorite story. And these are great costumes. Rented them for half off — even before Halloween."

"Who else would want them?" she asked, fingering the cheesy fabric of hers. "Forget about it. I'm not going dressed in this."

She went back to the table and began to clear. "You ready for dessert?"

"I'm always ready for dessert," he announced. That was certainly true.

Pete actually helped her take dishes off the table, a historic first. "What can I do to talk you into going with me? We'll have a great time."

She carefully stacked dishes in the sink, squirted in some soap, and turned on the water. "I might consider it if you got some reasonable costumes."

He stood right behind her, nuzzling her in that spot on the nape of her neck that blockaded thought processes. "Come on, Gwynnie," he purred. "Do this for me. It's always been my fantasy to be Peter Pan and get it on with Tinkerbell."

She felt herself falter. Playing Tinkerbell to Peter Pan had never been one of her fantasies, but maybe if she went along with his, he might go along with some of hers... Or at least the ones she felt comfortable talking about with him. Gwyn's mind wandered to her other fantasies. Romance with a capital R, as some tall, dark, handsome masked stranger swept her off her feet and carried her away to his palace. After a romantic meal served by impeccable retainers, the tall, dark, handsome man would take her to his most secluded chamber and...

With a wrench she forced her mind back to the present. She leaned back into Pete's kisses. "It's really one of your fantasies for us to go dressed as Peter Pan and Tinkerbell?" she asked.

"Yeah," he admitted. "And Gwyn, if you go to this with me, I promise I won't give you a hard time next time you want to go to one of your friends' fancy dress dinner parties."

"You'll wear a suit and tie without whining?"

He grinned. "I'll keep the whining to a minimum."

"If you're willing to promise me you'll wear a suit and tie in exchange, I know this means a lot to you. So, okay. I'll wear the Tinkerbell costume."

"Great," he said, moving away from her. "We can go to the party, then come back here in our costumes and…" His face lit up. He rubbed his hands together briskly. "So where's that dessert?"

"Why don't you make the coffee, and I'll get the tiramisu."

"You know I can't make coffee worth a darn." He lounged against the wall near her refrigerator.

"It's not rocket science," she said. "Watch me. You can start making coffee for the mornings when you're here for breakfast." She ground the beans, explaining each step. Then she started the coffee brewing and got the tiramisu out of the refrigerator. She arranged portions on little dessert plates. When the coffee was ready, she brought it all to the table.

By the time she lifted her fork for her first mouthful, Pete had already gobbled down his whole serving. "Got any more?" he asked, eyeing hers.

"Here, Pete. I'll give you some of mine. But savor it," Gwyn said. "Taste how good it is. Roll it around your tongue." She passed some her dessert to him.

He waggled his eyebrow. "I'd rather roll my tongue around something else."

Sounded good to her, but she wanted to finish her tiramisu first. "So tell me more about this party. Who else did you say is going?" Even though he'd raced through the fabulous confection, she intended to enjoy every last drop of her portion.

"Loads of people. Dominic Laredo has a huge yacht with a great big party room. So everyone from the San Diego branch of the company and other business associates are going to come together."

"Sounds like that guy needs to get a life instead of sailing around and forcing people to dress funny for parties."

Pete laughed. "I need to tell people that one. I'm surprised you don't know more about Dominic Laredo. They call him the playboy billionaire entrepreneur. Always going out with movie stars and lady senators and famous people. He was on a glossy magazine's Fifty of the Sexiest Guys in the Universe list last year."

"I must have missed that." She furrowed her brow in thought, intrigued in spite of herself. "Maybe this party will be better than I expect," she said. "And maybe I can fix up the costume, make it look less cheesy."

He frowned. "I think it'll look great on you as it is. I have an idea. Try it on. I bet you'll look really good—lots better than you expect."

That might not be a bad idea. If he saw how stupid she looked, maybe Pete would give in and let her get something more glamorous—or at least less embarrassing. She took the garment bag into her bedroom.

After she wriggled into the strapless costume Gwyn realized it was even skimpier than she'd first thought. Her boobs were hanging out the top. As for the bottom…she was grateful she'd gone for a recent bikini wax. Pete's eyes nearly popped out when she came back to the living room.

"I really can't go out in this," she said, making an it's-impossible gesture with her hands that almost left her nipples exposed. "I'd probably break several laws wearing this in public," she said.

"There'd be a line of guys waiting to bail you out," Pete said, twirling Gwyn around. "Why don't you put your hair up the way Tink always wears it?"

"You mean in a bun like in the cartoon?"

He snapped his fingers. "Yeah. Similar to the way you had it when I got here tonight only without the rose. And she wears those high little shoes with the fluff on the front."

"I'd feel more like a Playboy Bunny than Tinkerbell," she said.

"Hey, that works too. Speaking of being a Playboy Bunny, why don't we start making like two rabbits and…"

"I thought you wanted to do Peter Pan and Tinkerbell. You're not in costume."

"Tomorrow," he said, taking her in his arms.

"Be careful of my wings," Gwyn warned, as she let herself fall into his embrace.

"I'll be very careful," he said hoarsely as he slipped his fingers under the flimsy fabric. It took him just moments to slide the top of the costume off her breasts. Her nipples beaded before he pulled her to him, lowered his head, and began to suckle her left breast.

Gwyn ran her fingers through his hair as his tongue laved her nipple, sparking a live wire from her breast to her clit. Pete knew so many of the moves that were just right to bring her to the near shore of ecstasy. But she wanted to get to the far shore too. She moaned, wanting him to clamp his mouth down harder, to flick his tongue faster. With his left hand, he played with her right nipple, stroking, pulling, then cupping the breast. She wished he had two tongues. The thought brought her arching closer to him.

"Let's take this to the bed," he said dreamily.

For once, she undressed faster than he. All she needed to do was slip the clingy pink stuff off and step out. Maybe there were some advantages to the tiny costume.

Pete had his shoes and shirt off. His large erection was complicating the removal of his jeans. Gwyn decided to help. She ran her hand along Pete's fully packed rod, enjoying the feel of it as it bowed out the tracks of the zipper. "Let's get these pants off you," she whispered.

"Oh, yeah," he said.

She knelt down and began to finger the zipper, eliciting a major groan from him. "I need you to get it out, fast," he whimpered, hopping from foot to foot.

She started to ease the zipper over his bulge. He hissed when she caught a bit of flesh in the teeth, and she winced. She finally got the zipper down over the rest quickly, relieved to see that the minor mishap had done nothing to dampen Pete's ardor.

"Let me kiss it and make it better," she murmured.

"Oh, yeah, baby," he said as she took his engorged tip into her mouth and began to lick. He still stood with his jeans open, his throbbing shaft reaching out from the fly of his Batman shorts. While she lowered his jeans and shorts, she let her tongue explore him first, little darting flickers. She cupped his balls, stroking and squeezing as she licked the length of his cock, alternating that with taking the head in for a good solid suck.

He held her head to him, his fists buried in her hair. He made little, unintelligible noises and great big moans. "Gwynnnn," he groaned. "Oh, God. Jesus. So good."

She was really getting into it. He tasted and smelled of musk and Ivory soap, also salt and garlic—must have been the sauce. Tonight she suddenly decided, she was going to let him come in her mouth. Usually she didn't. Actually, she never had before. She knew he wanted to. And tonight, she wanted to cross that new bridge with him as a token of their relationship deepening. Tonight she would taste him as he let go in the release she brought him to. Tonight he'd be inside her in a new way. Another level of intimacy between them, opening them up to more of the romance she craved. And then maybe she'd be free to talk about some more of what she really wanted with him and get him to listen.

Now she let her teeth follow where her tongue and lips led, covering his cock with the tiniest of love bites, nips like from a butterfly's wings—or a magic fairy's. Maybe there really was something to her dressing up in the costume he'd picked.

She felt him grow larger in her mouth. She withdrew for a moment and then surrounded his balls with her lips, first one side then the other, tonguing and licking and showering him with more of the tiny love bites, all the while she stroked his moistened shaft with her eager fingers.

"Oh, Gwyn. You're killing me," he hissed. His hands gripped her tighter, as he bucked his hips to meet her mouth. "If we don't stop now and get next to each other, I'm going to…"

She pulled away and looked up at him from under lowered lashes. "That's what I want tonight," she murmured. "I want you come in my mouth. I want to taste all of you."

"Christ," he moaned as she took his cock back in her mouth and fingered his balls. They both began to move faster, her tongue and teeth urging him on, one hand on his ass, holding him to her.

He grew larger and harder and then screamed out as he began to pour himself into her mouth. Gwyn swallowed the salty bitter drops as Pete shuddered to the end of his climax.

Spent, he collapsed backward onto the bed.

Now Gwyn wanted to cocoon herself in Pete's arms and tell him how close to him she felt at this moment. She figured they'd talk a bit, cuddle, make love again—this time with her finally having the climax she'd been chasing all night—and fall asleep in each other's arms. And at some point, she'd start talking with him about exactly what she needed and wanted from him so clearly that he had to understand.

Pete lay back for about two minutes. Then he stood up. Gwyn stood up with him. She figured he'd finish undressing, get naked like she was.

Instead, Pete said, "Wow. That was really something," and proceeded to pull up his boxers and his jeans and zip himself shut.

Gwyn looked at him in surprise. She sat down on the bed and drew the top sheet around her. "What are you doing, Pete?"

He shrugged. "Gotta go, babe," he said.

She frowned. "Go? Where are you going?" Her voice rose in disbelief.

"I'm meeting some of my buddies. We got some underground Halloween horror videos. They've gotta go back tomorrow. Didn't I tell you?" He was fully dressed now.

"No. You neglected to mention your other plans." She let out an exasperated sigh. "I thought for sure you'd stay the night, like you usually do when you come here for dinner. I need you to stay." Her voice sounded to her like a whine, and she winced.

"Sorry," he said. He ran his index finger around her face. "Tomorrow night," he said. "Peter Pan and Tinkerbell. All night. I promise."

"I'm really disappointed," she said, wishing she knew a stronger word, wondering what he'd have done if she hadn't sucked him to climax. Wishing for a moment she was the kind of woman who could pick up her lamp and her bottles of perfume and throw them at him. Most of all, she wanted him to change his mind. But she knew he wasn't going to.

"I really need to go," he said. He hugged her. "Tonight was great. Great food, great sex." He gave her a good buddy tap on the rear. "And I promise one hundred percent I'll make it up to you tomorrow."

Her fists clenched, Gwyn watched Pete leave, whistling as he walked. Running on empty, Gwyn finished cleaning up from dinner and their brief interlude in the bedroom. Tonight felt like a rerun of too many previous nights.

No way she was going to be able to sleep 'til she at least took the edge off. Gwyn took a cold shower. She started getting into her cotton nightshirt, then reached for a red silk slip instead—one she'd wanted to wear with Pete. She lay down in bed and ran her hands up and down her breasts and belly, savoring the touch of the smooth fabric barely separating her fingers from her body. Her nipples hardened instantly as her fingers made contact with the sensitive puckers. She closed her eyes and fantasized Pete there with her, but Pete's face kept fading away. She must have been really pissed at him to keep losing his face in shadows the way she did. Instead, her dark, mysterious stranger came to her, cuffed hand and foot to a big bed. So he wouldn't be able to just run away. Spread eagle, with a huge erection she was about to lower herself on. Ooh, he was huge. As she humped him, he writhed, thrusting into her in a rhythm that...

Her right hand soon found its way down to her damp folds and her aching nub. She rubbed in all the places she was dying to have touched, the places the mysterious stranger was bringing to life as he moved. She clamped her thighs around her hand, two fingers now moving inside her as she pressed against her thumb. She pumped harder, harder...

Stronger measures were needed. Sighing, she reached into her night table drawer for her brand new deluxe vibrator, eight inches of creamy white plastic complete with a fresh battery. Guaranteed nirvana. She turned the vibrator on, pressed it against her cheek, and felt for just a moment the hum of its love song. She closed her eyes and invited her bound stranger back into the bed. He sang to her with the buzz of the vibrator. Oh, yes.

Foreplay was over. She put the vibrator where it belonged and rode that sucker like it was a bucking bronco and she a rodeo queen—within moments achieving the elusive climax she'd been primed for all night. Near tears with relief, Gwyn stroked her mollified folds and clit, ran her fingers through the blonde curls at the entrance of her core. The stranger was gone. She'd have liked him to stay longer.

One to take the edge off, but the need for release began to build in her again. She touched her wetness, then used her fingers to coat the vibrator with her dew. Marking her territory, she thought. She sniffed the vibrator, savoring her own scent—a delight Pete was missing out on tonight. She wondered idly if her scent turned him on, the way his scent did her. She licked the vibrator, tasting herself on its tip. Then she gave it a kiss, and directed it back to its primary duty.

Now she could take her time, allowing the vibrator's pulses to take her up the slope of sensation at a more leisurely pace. She closed her legs and opened them, comparing the different sensations she got from the tip of her plastic friend and the sides. Her orgasm snuck up on her. Suddenly, there it was, and there she was. At least with her vibrator and its heavy-duty battery, she knew she wouldn't be cut off in mid-come. She released a huge sigh, as her coordinated movements brought her to that second larger release she'd been thirsting for.

Thank the universe and the battery makers, she was at last relaxed. Gwyn hugged a pillow to herself and wondered about all her efforts to bring romance into her relationship with Pete. Was she fighting a losing battle, barking up the wrong tree? There was a lot she liked about Pete, but maybe what they did have together just wasn't ever going to be enough.

Alone at night like this, she could allow other desires free play, dreams of that dark stranger with an inventory of toys and experience she could only begin to imagine. She envied her clients, already in confidential communication with Fantasia Resorts about the fantasies they wanted to live out on their vacations. Gwyn had memorized the resort's brochures; she knew Fantasia Resorts was totally dedicated to the fulfillment of secret fantasies—as long as those were legal and involved only consenting adults. Every detail was seen to: food, service, décor, costumes, implements. There was even a joke that Fantasia Resorts controlled the weather. How ironic that Pete should work as one of the programmers who made sure those fantasies could be accommodated. He never appeared to have the slightest curiosity about anything but the most ordinary sexual activities—and he seemed to take all sensuous accompaniments for granted.

Gwyn tossed in bed, waiting to fall asleep. Her mother, always on the lookout for the man of her dreams, had abandoned Gwyn at age twelve—and disappeared from her life. Word was she'd followed the wrong man and ended up badly. Gwyn was raised from that time on by her mother's older sister Aunt Nora, a "spinster" who encouraged her to go to college, build a career, get secure, and avoid bad boys who'd lead her astray. But a French film Gwyn had snuck out of the house to see when she was thirteen always stuck in her mind and dreams as a model of passion and ecstasy. Erotic bondage and role play. Bad boys galore. Gwyn had burned with curiosity for years, but she'd always feared where that curiosity could lead. She wanted to be like Aunt Nora, but was afraid that deep down she was really more like her mother. If Gwyn let herself go, she'd follow the wrong man to disaster. Never mind that she'd have a great time 'til she got to disaster... So many thoughts swirled through her aching mind before she fell into a deep, dreamless sleep.

# Hook, Wine & Tinker

\* \* \* \* \*

Ready for bed in his luxurious quarters on board his yacht, Dominic Laredo reviewed his plans for the Halloween party he'd be hosting the next night. He stretched out his hands across the expanse of fine linen covering the king size custom mattress. The gentle lulling of the waves rocked his small world, bringing him to the edge of sleep. He'd set up these private quarters as the stage for his meeting with the woman of his fantasies. Of course he was always setting the stage for this woman to come into his life — in all his residences, at all his resorts. So far *she* hadn't, though hundreds of others had.

He began to stroke the erection that thoughts of his fantasy woman always brought. He grinned, wondering what the magazine that labeled him a sex god would think if they knew he'd taken himself in hand tonight.

There'd been many, many women in his life already. Being young, rich, and presentable meant having lots of potential playmates. It would have been no trouble finding one to share his bed tonight. His erection grew as he thought about the attractive company rep of a new catering service who'd made it clear she'd be happy to warm his bed. But taking the rep, Laura was her name, up on her offer would have obligated him to invite her to the party and focus his attention on her. And he wanted to be free for tomorrow night. His gut told him his fantasy woman might be there — and he knew for sure that Laura wasn't the one he'd been waiting for.

He stroked harder, amused at this way of satisfying himself that harked back to his first brushes with puberty — and his first thoughts of his dream woman. Dominic had been the quintessential nerd all through his early life in a small village in northern England, his years at school and at university. Bookish, skinny, shy, he'd used all his free time and roiling energy to learn everything he could about pleasing women. That was when he first conceived of his fantasy woman. All that book knowledge had served him well when he started his business. In a surprisingly few years, Fantasia Resorts had made him ridiculously wealthy and, as they say, he'd cleaned up real well. He'd achieved everything he'd ever dreamed of and more—but the woman he'd visualized sharing it all with still eluded him.

Hope sprang eternal. He'd know who she was by some synchronicity—of their looking up at the stars at the same moment, of the meeting of their hands while reaching for the same book from a bookstore rack, some sign. Being alone like this, whacking off, was a potent reminder of his past—and the dreams still waiting for fulfillment.

The down side of his success had been losing his sense of wonder. At thirty-two, he was in serious danger of becoming really jaded. He needed to be with someone new, fresh, someone capable of helping him rediscover zest. He'd been searching for the right woman, enjoying the search. But now he was ready to find her and change both their lives. Dominic was nothing if not an optimist. He was sure she'd come soon. Just like him.

## Chapter Two

Gwyn didn't feel any better about her costume when she put it on the next night to get ready for her date. And Pete was twenty minutes late picking her up. But once he got there, she had to admit he looked pretty damned good in his green tights and tunic. Especially those tights. They molded his buns, making them look higher and tighter than his usual jeans. Hmm. Maybe there was something to men in tights. Pete's tunic brushed his bulge, drawing her gaze like a neon bull's eye. She felt so hot looking at him, she lost her fear of freezing in the skimpy costume.

Pete gave her a gratifying up and down scan before grabbing her into a bear hug and deep searing kiss of thanks.

Mmm, she thought. Good start. She pressed herself against his bulge and relished his stiffening in response. His cock wedged against her folds beneath the thin fabric provided tantalizing friction. Maybe they could just forget about the party and…

He broke away from her. "Oh, baby, Peter thinks his Tink looks great."

She hated it when he spoke about himself in third person.

"Turn around," he ordered. "Let me see you flap your wings."

She slowly circled, letting him get an eyeful of more than just her wings, which quivered as she took tiny steps perched on her stiletto sandals.

"Yeah," he said when she'd completed her circle. She looked at his crotch to gauge his level of arousal. In those tights, he looked permanently good to go.

Pete looked at his watch. "We've got to get off to the marina."

Gwyn leered at him. "I thought we could maybe explore what's below those tights before we go to the party." She began to stroke him through the green nylon, bringing his cock to full attention.

Pete moaned, but pulled away, taking his rod out of her reach. "Oh, baby. No can do right now. Can't be late to the boss's party. I promise, later."

Gwyn promised herself she would not end the night with only her vibrator bringing her to glory. "You're the one who was late picking me up," she pointed out.

He held up a hand. "I know. My fault. But we need to get moving."

Carefully adjusting her wings, Gwyn slipped on her black silk cloak and followed Pete down to his vintage Jeep. Traffic flowed fairly smoothly, and they were soon parked in the lot closest to the dock where Dominic Laredo's yacht, the Bound for Pleasure, lay moored. Gwyn briefly wondered about that name. Bound for Pleasure. What did it mean? She grinned as the name sparked thoughts of her most inner fantasies... Could Dominic Laredo be referring to bondage...or did bound here merely mean a direction? Or could it be both? She found herself intrigued by the man she was about to meet. Of course she'd probably barely get a glimpse of him. He'd be surrounded by the usual rich man's entourage. If he even showed up for the party at all.

At their first sight of the yacht, Gwyn nearly joined Pete in his wolf whistle. She'd never been on a yacht before. Despite what Pete had told her about the large number of people who'd be attending, she'd expected it to be a somewhat small craft. What they were boarding resembled a floating palace, lit up like jewels rivaling the moon and starlight.

"Your boss has some taste in toys," Gwyn said to Pete. She preceded him as they climbed the gangplank to the deck, where vampires and witches, ghosts, skeletons, and zombies hobnobbed with ladies of the night and fairy tale ogres. Tuxedoed servers wearing simple masks circulated among the guests with platters of hors d'oeuvres and flutes of champagne.

"Looks like everyone's here already," Pete said, indicating the crowd.

"Looks like everyone's wearing a lot more clothes than I am," Gwyn whispered, feeling the absence of adequate cover and a mask. "Even the women dressed as hookers. I'm going to keep my cloak on."

"Aw, don't," Pete pouted.

"Perhaps you'll allow me to assist with your cloak," a deep resonant voice said from behind Gwyn, raising goose bumps up and down her spine as warm breath caressed the nape of her neck. Gwyn resisted the impulse to pat stray blonde curls into place to protect the delicate spot where she felt the mysterious speaker's gaze linger. At the same time, she was glad she'd worn her hair up. She turned slightly to see who was speaking.

"It's him," Pete whispered to Gwyn. "Dominic Laredo." Gwyn reached out and grasped Pete's arm to keep from wobbling in her high heels. So much for her speculation that she probably wouldn't even catch a glimpse of their host all night. Dominic Laredo was standing well within her comfort zone, demonstrating the truth of the expression *he bowled me over*. Gwyn really wished she had a mask. Fortunately, she knew she was far too insignificant in the scheme of things to register on Dominic Laredo's radar screen.

"Pete Payne from the local office," Pete said, propping Gwyn up with one hand and holding the other out to his host.

"Payne, of course. Introduce me to your companion," the other man commanded in a soft voice. Gwyn had not expected Dominic Laredo to have the cultured British accent of some Cambridge professor.

"This is my date, Gwyn Verde. Tinkerbell for tonight," Pete said. "I'm Peter Pan. Tink, uh Gwyn, this is Dominic Laredo. The man who thought up the concept of Fantasia Resorts."

Gwyn struggled to control her spontaneous attraction to the man, which instantly brought her a rush of heat and flashbacks of the forbidden French film from her youth. She was sure her face must be bright flaming red. So this was the person behind the vacations she ranked at the top of her wish list. The man sizing her up was the quintessential buccaneer: Tall and clean shaven, dark gray eyes gleaming with menace, long black hair tied back in a pony tail under an elegant tricorne, a gold hoop suspended from his right ear, and a plastic hook attached to one sleeve of his ornate jacket. Well, quintessential except for the hook being plastic. "How perfect your costume is," he purred. "And your ESP. I've come in my Captain Hook regalia—and you're just the one I've been looking for."

He was gazing directly at her when he said this. Pete just stood there, grinning. Probably thrilled to have another character from his favorite story there.

"Pleased to meet you," Gwyn stammered. Her insides were roiling—and it wasn't from the gentle rocking of the yacht. She held her hand out to the pirate captain, who surrounded her trembling fingers with his large warm palm. She looked questioningly at his plastic hook.

He laughed. "Don't worry. For tonight, I'm using my party hook instead of the real one," he said so softly she had to lean toward him to hear. "I keep my real one in my quarters. I'll be happy to show it to you."

She pulled her hand out of his embrace. From resenting her part in the silly charade she'd agreed to play, she'd suddenly advanced to feeling trapped in a dangerous role. What *had* happened between Tinkerbell and Captain Hook? She couldn't remember—and she couldn't believe she was asking herself that question.

"I really would be happy to take personal charge of your cape," he said. "It will be safe with me." His voice lingered on the word *safe*.

Gwyn clutched the cape tighter. She wanted to pull it around herself and hide away from his gaze in an obscure corner of the huge room. But she needed to act like a reasonable adult. So she said, "Thank you. It's a bit chilly, so I'd like to keep it for now."

He inclined his head slightly as he looked at her from under hooded eyes. "Your wish is my command. And now, if you'll excuse me, I will see to my other guests."

As soon as he'd drifted away, Gwyn was relieved to feel her heartbeat slow down and her breathing return to normal.

"I think he likes you," Pete said, looking enormously pleased.

For just a moment, she'd forgotten him.

"Let's eat," he said, leading the way to where a server was handing out shish-kebabs of meat, mushrooms, tomatoes, and onions.

Gwyn's throat had knotted up. She didn't think she could swallow a bite of anything. Maybe she'd be better off drinking something before she attempted to eat. She reached for a champagne flute from a passing tray.

\* \* \* \* \*

Dominic said hello to a major vendor and his wife who'd driven down from L.A. The wife prattled on about how great the food was, how gorgeous and luxurious the yacht. Of course.

*She* was here tonight. She'd come to his party, just as he'd been sure she would. Dominic could scarcely keep his mind on greeting his guests. How perfect that she'd come dressed as Tinkerbell when he'd chosen to be Captain Hook. Synchronicity.

Dominic lifted a champagne flute and toasted her from across the room, pleased to see her mirroring his movements though she wasn't looking his way.

Her body had signaled to him like a faithful compass the moment she entered his space. He'd sensed her before he'd fully seen her, heard her words, touched her. Each new layer of sensation added to his assurance that she would be his before the party ended. How perfect that she was on the Bound for Pleasure tonight.

She was beautiful, of course. He longed to undo the sexy blond bun, rub his face in the wispy tendrils escaping her sparkling tiara. He'd have to get that cape away from her so he could really feast his eyes on her body—which a glimpse of trim ankles promised would far exceed his fantasies. He felt himself begin to harden and took pleasure in how his needs and hers would unite them—soon.

His erection grew, pressing against his pirate breeches, as he watched Tinkerbell, her name was Gwyn Verde, turn to, what was his name?, Payne. Dominic almost groaned at the thought of her with him. Payne had some skills that made him tolerable in his minor position in the company. Reports from his resource people labeling Payne as immature and lacking true initiative told Dominic loud and clear this man would never rise beyond a mid-level position.

So why was the beautiful woman of his dreams with Payne?

Dominic normally would have rejected the possibility of going after any other man's woman, especially an employee's.

Except that the man she was with was totally wrong for her. No. That was the wrong way to analyze the situation. He, Dominic Laredo, was the only *right* man for her. He had to make sure she knew it—pronto.

He drained his champagne and began to move in her direction.

\* \* \* \* \*

One flute of champagne did not suffice to untie the knot in Gwyn's throat, so she reached for a second. She was beginning to feel ridiculous as she stood clutching her cape with her left hand and guzzling champagne with her right. She probably had more people staring at her draped in her cape than would have if she finally took the darn thing off and just swaggered around the room with a confidence she didn't feel.

Pete was waving to some guys dressed as Super Heroes. "Gwyn, I just need to go talk to my buddies over there about our football pool. Kind of stuff that bores you, I know. Why don't you grab yourself something to eat, and take off the cape? Later, I want to show you off." He grinned. Before she could say anything, he made his way across the crowded room and began clapping Spiderman on the back.

Great, she thought, finishing her second, unaccustomed champagne. She felt tipsy, abandoned, and far too warm to continue wearing the cloak. Maybe she'd try to find Dominic Laredo and let him put it away for her. On second thought, finding him was probably not a good idea. She felt that if she took off her cape in front of him, big red neon arrows pointing to her clit from all directions would light up and demonstrate his effect on her.

Better she should avoid Dominic Laredo, who made her think of turbaned charmers playing flute music for snakes to rise and undulate to. She gulped. Even thinking of looking for him must mean she was beyond tipsy.

She could strangle Pete for leaving her stranded like this. He knew she was shy in large groups of people she didn't know. Last she'd seen, he'd still been gabbing away with his friends. And people said women talked a lot. Pete probably wouldn't even miss her if she took off.

Gwyn was in danger of losing her last drop of patience with the man. She just wanted to go home, forget this night, and cut her losses. Seeing Pete cavorting with the Hulk and Spiderman while she seethed in misery really had to be a wake-up call on his potential as a future anything that involved sensitivity and a recognition of her needs.

When she'd had enough, Gwyn went over to where Pete and the Super Heroes were huddled together. "Pete," she said when she finally snagged his attention, "still busy with your friends?"

Pete put a proprietary arm around her. "Gwyn, Spiderman here is Roger and the Hulk is Chuck. Guys, this is Gwyn."

The two men grunted greetings.

"Are you still talking about football?"

Pete chuckled. "Yeah, a bit of a problem about our pool. Say guys, where are your ladies?"

Spiderman shrugged. "Linda is off somewhere with Tina. They wanted to look at the light fixtures or something. Linda's dressed like Little Bo Peep, and Tina like a hooker."

"Interesting combination," Gwyn said.

Pete turned to her. "Why don't you go look for them? You all can chat while me and the guys settle things about the pool. Be much more interesting for you."

"Okay, but we really need to talk soon," Gwyn said, trying to communicate with her eyes that she was serious.

"Soon, I promise. But we've gotta finish working this out now." He gestured to his two buddies, who nodded.

Not pleased, Gwyn gave up on Pete for now and went in search of the female twosome. After all, how hard could it be to find a Bo Peep walking with a hooker?

Pretty hard. After circulating all over the room for fifteen minutes, she gave up and headed back to Pete. He was still immersed in his conversation, oblivious to her. That was it—the last straw. She reached into the pocket of her cape for her tiny bag and pulled out her cell phone. She'd get a cab to come out and rescue her. Thank goodness she'd brought money. Previous nights out with Pete had taught her to be prepared. When she connected with a dispatcher, she found out she'd have to wait a half hour and pay a bundle to get home. An expensive lesson, but anything was worth never having to repeat a night like this one.

It would probably be best to get sober before she attempted to make her way down the gangplank. Figuring she'd better eat to counteract what she'd drunk, she turned around to take a crab-stuffed mushroom from a passing server. She'd just bitten into the mushroom and was savoring its rich herbs when *he* was standing at her elbow.

"Gwyn," he said, devouring her with those dark eyes, "you look flustered. Is something wrong?"

She gulped down the mushroom. The last thing on earth she wanted right now was to tell him the truth. But as she tried to think of a way to fluff him off, she looked deep into his amazing gray eyes and felt compelled to come up with some plausible story. "I, uh, am not feeling real good. Thought it would be best to go home. I just called a cab. I don't want to drag Pete away from the party this early."

Dominic frowned. "I'm sorry you're not feeling all right. Has something here at the party bothered you—something you've eaten or drunk?"

She shook her head. "Nothing like that. Everything here's wonderful. But I've been working a lot of extra hours lately. It's probably catching up with me."

He was so focused on every word she said. "Well, if you want to go home, I can have my driver take you. Though you might want to go somewhere quieter and just rest for a bit. Then you'd be able to stay longer." He thought for a moment. "In fact, why don't you come to my quarters. You can rest, see if you care to rejoin the party later. Cancel the cab."

"Oh, thank you," she said, blushing from his scrutiny. "It's really not necessary to go to so much trouble."

"No trouble at all. I insist." He looked her up and down. "You look very warm. That might be the problem. Why don't you take off that cape? Maybe you'll feel better immediately."

Stupid to keep resisting. "Thank you, Mr. Laredo," she said, starting to shrug it off when he stepped behind her. He caressed her neck lightly as he removed the cape, starting a riot in her bloodstream. She tried not to wobble on her heels.

"My friends call me Dominic," he said. "I consider all my guests to be friends."

"Dominic," she repeated shyly.

"You do Tinkerbell proud," he whispered.

"You really are very kind." Taking the cape off didn't cool her off a bit. Even in her skimpy costume, she could have sworn she'd landed in the middle of a heat wave. "I hate to put you to any inconvenience."

Dominic shrugged. "The party's in full swing. I'm sure no one would miss me for the few moments it'll take to escort you to my quarters."

"I really don't want to impose..."

"You're not," he assured her, steering her lightly through the throng to a nearby door. She longed to lean into his hand, which felt strong and hot at the small of her back.

Once out of the party room, Dominic took her to the deck, where some couples were taking advantage of the moonlight and the relative mildness of the night for more personal pursuits. Not wanting to disturb any of them, Gwyn followed Dominic in silence.

He led her through another door to a large cabin dominated by a huge bed. He indicated she should sit in an armchair and put her feet up on a footrest while he hung her cape carefully in a closet.

Gwyn looked around. The cabin was decorated in a style she'd label elegant masculinity, with many built-in cabinets of a dark wood like mahogany—and many mirrors. She saw herself reflected back, looking like a doe frozen by oncoming headlights as she perched at the edge of the wine-red leather chair with her bare feet extended on the matching footstool.

"You feeling any better?" he asked.

She nodded.

"Tell me which cab company you called, and I'll cancel for you."

"That's all right," she said. "I can do it." She took out her cell and contacted the company. When that was taken care of she asked, "Is this where you live?" As soon as her words were out, she bit her lips. She couldn't believe how inane she must sound.

"Sometimes." Dominic sat on the edge of the bed near her and reached for her hands. "I love spending time on the Bound for Pleasure. Must have had some seafaring ancestors. Alas, it's not practical for full time residence. So I have homes in New York, London, and Honolulu and, of course, here in San Diego. That's in addition to having small residences at all seven of the resort sites."

She raised her eyebrows at this. She'd known he was rich, but having all those homes made the information concrete. "As a travel agent, I send many clients to Fantasia Resorts."

"I knew I had a good reason for being grateful to you," he grinned. "Perhaps some day you'll take a holiday at one of our resorts yourself."

"I dream of doing that — some day," she admitted. She didn't mention that she'd have to hit a lottery jackpot before that could happen.

"Let me know, any time. I'd see to your accommodations personally. In fact, we can talk about your holiday ideas tonight or the next time we're together."

That's how he'd gotten so rich, Gwyn thought. He was very good at what he did, so easily reading her mind as to what she wished for. And too sexy. She drew back. He was talking about some other time. As if the two of them would ever see each other again after tonight. A sense of unease began to battle with her growing desire for him.

She put her feet on the floor and started to stand up out of the armchair. "Maybe I should be getting back to the party. Pete is probably looking for me." He probably wasn't. She'd have to figure out another way to get home, especially after she'd cancelled her taxi.

"Of course," he said, rising, "if you're feeling better." He gazed at her and suddenly appeared to get a new idea. "Maybe you'd like to see my real hook before you go. The one I'm not wearing tonight. May I show it to you?"

She raised an eyebrow in surprise. She'd thought he'd been joking about the plastic hook taking the place of a real one. She shivered deliciously at the prospect of a real hook.

"You actually have one?" she asked, giving a little nervous laugh.

"I take role play very seriously, just like all my other play," he said. "You need to be sure you have all the props and whatever else you require for it to work."

"I guess I'd never thought about play that way," she said.

He studied her for a moment. "I think you have," he said softly. "Or maybe that's just my imagination working overtime. Come, my Tinkerbell. Let me show you my captain's hook."

"Okay," she said. "But then I really need to leave."

"As you wish."

Trembling, she let him take her hand and lead her over to one of his cabinets. He turned a small white porcelain knob and opened a door. Gwyn gasped. Inside was a sheet of dark wood with many hangers displaying a diverse collection of gleaming metal. Gwyn saw various hooks and also what looked like handcuffs and other implements she couldn't name. Her heartbeat accelerated and she swallowed hard. As she surveyed the highly polished contents, Gwyn couldn't help wondering what all those things were—and if they had any use aside from show.

From one hanger Dominic took…a hook. The metal arc was attached to a piece of wood. Gwyn touched it gingerly with a kind of horrified fascination. "Is this a *real* one?"

He smiled. "Do you mean is this what Captain Hook might have used in place of his missing hand?"

She nodded, running her fingers over the cold surface of the metal and the polished wood.

"Be careful, Gwyn. It's very sharp at the point—and I don't want you to get hurt."

She pulled her hand back.

"You can touch it again," he said. "Just be careful. And yes, this is the kind of device people used to use."

"Why do you have it?" she asked, her mouth dry.

He chuckled dryly. "Curious, are you?"

She nodded.

"I found it at one of my favorite antique shops in London. Felt I needed an authentic Captain Hook hook to add to my collection of goodies. So far, I've never used it in any play. Can't quite figure out how to hide my own hand and carry the hook without injuring people around me."

"Oh," she said. "But why would you especially want a Captain Hook hook? Almost everybody roots for Peter Pan."

He nodded. "But Gwyn, I've never been one to root for everyone else's favorite. Not without a good reason."

"You go your own way, then?"

"Exactly," he said. "I'm always fascinated by the dark side of the story. Sometimes that's where the true heroes reside. Or at least the really fascinating characters. I think that may be the case for the Peter Pan story, don't you?"

Gwyn had never thought that way. Captain Hook as the hero—or at any rate, the most interesting character—of the story? A little scary, but definitely...tantalizing. But she didn't want to let him know the direction of her thoughts, so she tried to pull back to some more neutral conversation. "Your collection is quite impressive," she said, indicating the other implements displayed.

"Thank you." He put the hook back in its place and looked at her as if to ask if that was all she was going to say. After several beats of silence, he asked, "Anything else you'd like to look at?"

Despite her better judgment, she pointed mutely to a pair of handcuffs.

He took them down and held them out to her.

"Why did you pick these?" he asked, as she reached out to touch them. The cool metal bit into her fingers with electric heat. Despite her shock, she maintained the contact—almost powerless to remove her fingers.

Gwyn couldn't tell him, this man she'd just met and who was her boyfriend's boss, that she'd always had fantasies about handcuffs—though she suspected he knew. In addition to wanting to jump his bones, she was starting to feel she could say anything to him, tell him her deepest, darkest desires, and nothing she could say would surprise or shock him... Maybe making people feel like that was at the heart of what he did for his business. She could very easily imagine describing her fantasies to him—not to mention living them out.

Reality check time, she reminded herself. Being here with this man was so not her. But she'd probably never again in her life be alone with a man like Dominic Laredo. Heck, they were ships passing on a moonlit Halloween night. So maybe she'd confide a little of her fantasy to him. He'd probably heard it all, lived it all.

"They're antique, aren't they?" she asked as she continued to caress the cuffs with her fingers. They really were quite beautiful, more ornate than the utilitarian ones she'd seen in movies and on TV.

"They are pretty old," he said. "But you didn't answer my question." He dared her to tell him her thoughts.

She sighed. She'd go for it, at least a little. Why not? "Sometimes I've thought about how it would be to be handcuffed with my lover..." she said, feeling her face flame red.

Dominic Laredo was now so close they were practically touching. She could feel the heat from his body reaching out and searing her. "Would you like to try that out now?" he whispered, and her body resonated like a bell in a windstorm.

She was going to protest that her lover wasn't there, but her mouth couldn't form the words. At this moment, the only possible lover on the horizon was Dominic Laredo. "Yes," she said, her voice barely rising above a whisper. However, mustering some reserve of inner "Aunt Nora" strength from deep in her gut, she put the cuffs down and picked up her cape. "But I won't." She took a deep breath. "I really need to leave. *Now.*"

She saw a flicker of surprise—or was it disappointment?—cross his face. But he didn't object or try to change her mind. Instead, he picked up the handcuffs and held them out to her. "Allow me to give you these as a gift."

Right. Like she could accept a gift from him, one that would keep her thinking of him for the rest of her life. Not to mention they were probably expensive—and a lady didn't accept expensive gifts from men she didn't know. "Thank you. But I couldn't." She clutched the cape so as to have something to do with her hands. "You've already shown me too much kindness, and I'm taking you away from your party." She slipped the cape on over her shoulders.

He moved away from her. "I suppose I should put in an appearance there. But Gwyn, why don't you stay here a bit longer, rest up. If you want, you can play with the handcuffs while I go fill my hostly duties."

She hesitated—and felt her resolve begin to melt away. "I really shouldn't," she said, her voice without conviction even to her ears.

"That's a word I've banished from my vocabulary," he said.

"What is?" she asked, curious.

"*Should*," he said, making a face. "And its evil counterpart *shouldn't*. By simply getting rid of those two words, I improved my life several hundred percent."

She laughed. "You're making that up."

"No," he said, looking very serious. "But if I still did allow myself to use that word, I'd say 'Gwyn, you *should* stay. I want you to, and I think you want to also.'"

He spoke, and her clit vibrated. He *couldn't* know that, could he? Dominic Laredo and his amazing handcuffs. How could she turn her back on this? But no way was she going to let him know what he was doing to her. So she willed herself to look cool. "All right," she said. "Just to try out those handcuffs for a bit because I'm curious about them."

He nodded. "And Gwyn, whenever you want to go home, if Payne is unavailable I'll have my driver take you."

"Fair enough," she said, feeling herself begin to relax as he left.

The handcuffs were amazing. She slipped her hands in, first the left, then the right, being sure to keep them open.

The cool metal around her wrist sparked a fantasy of being with Dominic Laredo, who looked a hell of a lot like the man in her fantasies. Though the warning voice inside her head that still used the word *should* insisted she leave now, she silenced it and gave in to her desire to linger.

\* \* \* \* \*

Dominic did not want to leave Gwyn, but he forced himself to. He figured that if he left her alone for a bit, she might unwind enough to follow her instincts—straight to him. And he did have an obligation to spend some time at his party with his other guests.

When he returned to the main room, the party was in full swing, people laughing and talking, the food and drinks flowing. Dominic spotted Payne in conversation with men in Super Hero costumes. He wondered if Payne had even noticed that Gwyn was gone. How could anyone take for granted having a lady like her in his life? Dominic realized he should say something to Payne about Gwyn.

He went over to the group, chatted with them all for a bit, then asked Payne to step away from the others for a moment. "Payne," he said. "Your friend, Miss Verde, is feeling unwell."

Payne/Peter Pan scowled. "She have one of her headaches?"

Dominic shook his head. "She hasn't told me the exact nature of her distress. She's resting right now."

"Okay," Payne said. "Whatever. As long as she's ready for the costume competition later. She looks dynamite, doesn't she?"

"I'll tell her what you said."

Dominic almost relished the idea of being Payne's messenger. It would give him a good pretext to get back to Gwyn quickly.

Everyone seemed to be having a great time—without him. He took some hors d'oeuvres on a plate for Gwyn. Fortunately he had a fully stocked bar in his cabin.

*****

Despite her best intentions, Gwyn had managed to get herself locked in the handcuffs. Great, she thought. Dominic Laredo would think she was a major klutz. Not that it mattered what he thought, she kept reminding herself. It was a fluke that she'd met him at all. Even though he spoke of their being together again, she knew being with him was a once in a lifetime event.

According to the vibes she was picking up, he found her attractive. She wasn't sure why he was paying so much attention to her. This guy was used to having any woman he wanted. Despite her self-affirmations, she had to admit she was ordinary—certainly not a movie star or supermodel type like he was used to. The thought of possibly spending time with him, having him as her lover... A fantasy worthy of his resort. Too rich for her blood. She needed to get the cuffs off and get her butt out of here. With or without Pete.

Her inner psychoanalyst chimed in with accusations. Maybe she'd locked herself in the cuffs for some deep psychological reason. Maybe it was her evil twin taking over, the part of her that wouldn't let go of the French film. For now, thanks to her stupid mistake, she was dependent on Dominic Laredo. Alone in his cabin. Handcuffed. She *should* be horrified, but somehow that was an emotion she couldn't come up with. Excited, yes. Twitchy with need, yes. Horrified, no.

She missed him, wanted him to return—fast. She could admit that much to herself.

And then she heard his footsteps in the hallway outside the door. She blushed when he came through the door and saw her, sure he could read her thoughts. It was too embarrassing to admit she'd locked herself in the cuffs—and also too delicious. Dominic Laredo was carrying a plate loaded with food—for her. When she saw him with the food, her traitor stomach grumbled. But more than the food, the moment she saw him again, she knew beyond any hesitation that she wanted him. She wanted to know what it would be like to make love with a man who had antique cuffs in his personal collection. More than that, she wanted to know what it would be like to have him inside her when her hands were inside those cuffs.

And she wanted to feel herself all over him when he lay cuffed beneath her. Even if it was only once in her lifetime.

"Please help yourself to something to eat," he said, putting the plate down on the small table next to her. He sounded so normal, being polite to her when her fantasies had him wild and primitive. Was it possible that the attraction was all one-sided and she was only imagining he wanted more than to be a polite host? If she was the only one getting overheated here, it would be even more embarrassing than getting stuck in the cuffs.

Well, no help for it. She had to show him her cuffed hands. Rolling her eyes, she held up her bound wrists and waited for him to laugh. He didn't.

Instead, he touched her gently. "I should have warned you about those cuffs. They lock so easily, people get caught all the time."

She raised her eyebrows. He used these cuffs all the time? Man, was she in over her head with this guy.

"I'll get the key," he said. He went over to a small drawer in his night table and took out a key. His left hand braced her elbow as he started to unlock the cuff with his right.

Gwyn could scarcely breathe, both from his touch on her arm and from her growing desire. Blushing harder, she whispered, "No. Not yet."

He looked at her like a starving man at a banquet, then removed the key and put it down.

"As long as I'm in the cuffs already..." Her eyes pleaded with him for what she couldn't find the words to ask for.

"Yes," he said.

She took a deep breath. "Please take me in your arms," she said, amazing herself at how hard it was for her to say the simple words of what she wanted from him. Her thoughts flickered to Pete, and she wondered if she was as unable to communicate what she really wanted with him as with Dominic Laredo.

"You want me to hold you?" he asked, the plate of food now long put aside and forgotten.

Still holding her cuffed hands up in front of her, she nodded mutely.

"You don't have to ask me twice," he said hoarsely. "As long as you're sure..."

"I am." Her words sounded quavery to her.

He took her in his arms, and the world disappeared. "Is this what you want?" he asked, putting his arms around her waist and pulling her close as she held her imprisoned hands up above her.

"Yes," she said, nearly cross eyed with the wonder of having him hold her so close.

He nuzzled her neck, spreading heat and light everywhere he touched with his lips, his breath. Gwyn felt something tightly held within her break loose, and she moaned her pleasure at his being with her, like this.

She opened her mouth to invite his kiss and lowered her cuffed wrists around his neck. His lips began a quick, hot exploration of her waiting mouth. His tongue danced with hers as he nibbled her lips, his hands everywhere. He smelled and tasted of soap, sea, and one hundred percent male. Gwyn tried to put everything she was feeling into her kiss, how hot she was for him. She felt as if all the oxygen had whooshed out of her, and the only way she'd ever have more would be to get it from him. They broke for air.

He looked at her from the circle of her arms. "Gwyn, hold that thought."

"What thought?" she asked, as incapable at that moment of thinking as of running an Olympics sprint.

He chuckled dryly. "I love your sense of humor. But please excuse me for one moment. Uh, that is if you'll raise your arms." Blushing that she'd held him prisoner, she raised her arms and watched hungrily as he crossed to the cabin door and turned a knob. He returned to her and hoarsely whispered, "Now we won't be interrupted. Gwyn, will you come to my bed, now?"

All she could do was slowly nod her assent and hold out her still cuffed hands.

"Let me help you out of those clothes," he purred.

Embarrassed to have to wriggle out of the Tinkerbell outfit and wings while she was handcuffed, glad she'd worn minimal underwear, hopeful that he wouldn't be disappointed with her in any way—with his big hands smoothing the way, Gwyn was nude in seconds flat—except for the cuffs and the tiny diamond studs in her ear lobes. "You are so amazingly beautiful," he murmured, drinking her in with his eyes. Dominic was still dressed, though the prominent bulge in his pants told Gwyn he'd rather be otherwise.

"Aren't you going to get naked too?" she asked, expectation and lust enabling her to find her tongue.

"Now it's your time," he said, running his hands over the handcuffs and her arms. "Are you sure this is still what you want?" he asked.

She nodded.

"You trust me so much, Gwyn? Even with the cuffs still on you?"

Trust. To her amazement, she found she could say yes.

He ran his hands down her face, then touched her hair. "How about if we let down your hair now?"

"My hair?" she asked.

"Yes," he murmured. "I've been wondering all night how your hair would look fanned out on my pillow."

"Oh," she said, wishing she'd regain her power of intelligent conversation sometime soon.

"And you'll be much more comfortable. Above all else, I want your comfort tonight."

His fingers made short work of the pins she'd used to make her Tinkerbell bun. When she felt her hair flow down her neck, she shook her head once or twice to try to clear it. And then she got into his bed.

\* \* \* \* \*

She was like every dream he'd ever had come true. And here she was, in his bed. Giving him everything—her luscious body, her openness to the new, but especially her trust.

Dominic eased Gwyn back among his pillows. He helped her raise her arms over her head, making her both as comfortable as someone whose hands were cuffed could be and available to him. Just as he'd imagined, her hair fanned out like a crown of sunshine across his pillow. He now had a clear view of her pert, firm breasts, her flat belly, her feminine core under its golden blond curls. He didn't know where to look first, wanted to look everywhere at once. But looking wasn't enough. He had to touch her, to possess her.

She was so amazingly beautiful and vulnerable to him, lying there. And so nervous and excited—he could feel her quivering. He felt his own rising anticipation, as if he were an inexperienced, horny adolescent. But now he could bring all he'd learned about satisfying a woman to their time together. With her, he'd rediscover the wonders of unfolding intimacy—and maybe some of the sense of newness long missing for him.

This first time, he would pleasure her. Though he was dying for his own release, he wanted her to know how much he treasured her. He would bring her the satisfaction she deserved and, if he could read women at all, needed. Dominic sensed Gwyn had never been loved as completely and thoroughly as he intended to love her.

He stretched out next to her, first just running his hands slowly over every inch of her body. She moaned from the butterfly flicker of his touch, just barely skimming over her skin. He watched how her nipples hardened when he touched them, first gently, then with more pressure as she pushed her perfect breasts against his questing fingers. Her nipples were a soft pink color, delicate. He nearly growled with joy as they blossomed and beaded when he at last took them in his mouth.

Dominic could have suckled at Gwyn's breasts all night, but so many other delights awaited. While he used his hand to play with her nipples, he watched as Gwyn opened her legs, revealing the damp pink folds beckoning him. He wanted to dive into her, but first he wanted her to desire him there. He longed for her to be crazy to have him there — to writhe and call out with her need. It was good, for their first time together, that he didn't cuff her legs. He'd postpone playing that way for another time. He was confident there would be many more times. There had to be, oh God, there had to be.

This awesome woman needed to have every inch of her attended to. Keeping his voice steady, Dominic whispered, "Would you please turn over? I want to see your back."

She groaned her response, her eyes half lidded with lust. As it was complicated for her to shift with her hands in the cuffs, he helped her move so that her gorgeous back was to him.

Smooth. He straddled her, his hard cock pressed against her back deliciously. Calling on his iron will and self-control, Dominic bit back his howl of joy. He had to concentrate on her, to put his own needs off to a remote corner of his feverish brain. But every moment they were together convinced him more and more that she was the woman he'd waited so long for.

Dominic placed his hands on her shoulders. He began to kiss and nibble at her, fisting his hand in her silky hair and lifting it so he could start at the nape of her swan-like neck, then tongue the sweet tendrils of blonde hair that escaped his fingers. Her skin tasted like the sweet cream it resembled. Sweet cream fragrant with roses and exotic eastern spices. She wriggled, pressing his cock with her tush so he thought he'd nearly burst with his own pleasure. Nearly cross-eyed with rock-hard driving need, he lifted his hips slightly from her to ease the pressure building in him.

He wouldn't leave a spot of her unexplored, untouched — he longed to claim every bit. Tongue, teeth, lips, fingers—all paid homage to the miracle of her soft skin. Her scent made him drunk, the different textures of her skin and the bones beneath brought his fingertips alive. He tasted her slowly as she ground her feminine mound into his bed, greeting his kisses with moans and gasps of passion.

When he reached her cheeks, two tight mounds of alabaster, he playfully kissed and nibbled the tight valley between them—causing her to gasp with surprise and try to move him away. "Not there," she said. "Please, don't kiss me or touch me there."

"Why not?" he asked, lifting his face while his fingers continued his exploration.

"It's embarrassing," she said, her voice sounding strained.

"Nothing about you is unpleasant," he said. "Every inch of you is perfection."

"You sure?" she asked.

"Oh, yes," he said, his tongue returning to the tiny hole.

Her buttocks tightened, telling him she still wasn't relaxed, but she didn't make any further protests. Nonetheless, he wanted her to continue trusting him, so he moved on to the folds between her thigh and her butt and let his tongue explore there. She relaxed, pressing up to meet his touch and his kiss.

He worked his way down her left leg, lavishing attention on the delicate skin behind her knee, massaging her firm leg muscles as he let his tongue and teeth and lips continue exploring. From the way she responded, he knew she'd never before been loved the way he was loving her.

Great as his pleasure was, knowing that he was taking her to new places made him even higher.

He moved on to her right leg, making sure he kissed this one as thoroughly as the left. Knowing how delicious they were, he'd kept the ankles and feet for last. As he tasted the soles of her feet, once again she protested with concern about smells and tastes — though not nearly as strongly as when he'd tongued her anus. Mostly she seemed to be savoring all the new sensations he was giving her. More than anything, he wanted to convince her that her tastes and scents enchanted him — and he tried to do so both by filling the room with his own moans and groans of pleasure and by repeatedly pressing his screaming cock against her. She had to feel how much what was happening between them turned him on.

When he'd saturated her with kisses, he helped her turn over again and started sucking her toes. Oh, she liked this. He lingered over each toe, especially the small ones, circling the base and then the tip with his tongue. Then he worked his way slowly up each foot and leg, massaging, burying his face between her thighs and her glistening folds. With superhuman will, he held back from touching her hungry pink core 'til he'd touched and kissed everywhere else. Because he knew, once he got to her cunt, he wouldn't ever want to leave.

From the top of her legs, he went back to her beautiful face. She responded with fire and light, nipping him back with her teeth, joining her tongue to his in a dance that left them both gasping. Her face, her neck, her breasts — with nipples as hard as his cock. He tongued under them, working his way down her flat belly, across her hips.

And then he was there, at her pussy, where he'd wanted to be since the moment they met. He buried his face in her folds, savoring the sweet musk. He ran his fingers along those folds, taking her wetness and sucking it from his fingertips. She had her legs open wide now, and she was whimpering for him to bring her to completion. Her cuffed hands moved with her as she writhed to close the minuscule distance between them.

He slowly slipped one finger into her, and she closed her legs around him, begging for more. Quickly, he slid a second finger into her, driving both deep inside. She rode his two fingers, working her legs to draw him even tighter and higher in her. Trying to ignore his throbbing cock, he lowered his head for his first kiss and taste of her swollen clit. She screamed his name and flung her legs into a vise-like grip around his head.

Christ, she was so hot, she felt like she'd combust any moment in an explosion that would rock his yacht and the whole marina. He teased her clit and folds with little flicks of tongue, inhaling her scent and taste as she thrust herself harder against him. She needed the long, languorous licks he planted in and on her rosy petals of flesh, his mouth now dripping with her juices.

She rode him, moving herself to meet his probing tongue, his kisses, his hot breath. Her sharp intake of breath told him she was probably moving up to the release she'd been begging for all night. He urged her on with his eager mouth and fingers, shuddering with her as she called out to him in a loud, trembling release.

They collapsed together.

"Thank you," she whispered when she had her breath.

"Oh, God," he said. She didn't need to thank him. He told her so. They both lay together in soft silence. Then she sat up a bit and said, "Dominic, your turn. Get out of those clothes."

He could deny her nothing. But he'd just begun to unzip his pants to liberate his aching cock when a loud noise intruded on their private moment. They looked at each other. What sounded like a small army was hammering on the door to Dominic's quarters.

"Open up!" someone shouted. They both froze.

# Chapter Three

As the racket from the hallway continued, Gwyn lay shattered in Dominic's bed. The noise distracted him from getting naked with her. He'd left her in the bed, and now she had time for her mind to go into its analytical games.

She'd never before done anything remotely like this. After coming with him, she realized she'd never really *had* an orgasm before. Now she wanted his cock in her, and she hated that they'd been interrupted.

From some deeply hidden corner of her mind, a message flashed that she should maybe feel guilty or bad or something. The *should* word again. She had to agree with Dominic on how much better her life would be if she could lose that word. *Should* was at war with the reality that she'd just had the most fantastic orgasm of her life in the bed of a man she'd barely met—for she was sure she *shouldn't* have let herself get to this position.

Even though it was a *great* position. She smiled wickedly to herself.

No matter how hard she tried, she couldn't scrape up even one iota of feeling bad or guilty. Not the tiniest speck. She couldn't conjure up any of those feelings. If she was supposed to have them—she *should* have them—too bad.

All she wanted right now was for the good feelings to continue and, especially, to give back to Dominic some of the pleasure he'd just showered her with.

Was it Dominic, or the handcuffs, or both?

Too much thinking—that was always her way. For now, she just wanted to surrender to feelings. And she wanted him there, with her, on her, in her. She wanted to feel his cock in her the way his tongue had been—and deeper than his tongue could go. Whatever happened after tonight, she didn't care. She wanted him in her. Now.

What was that noise at the door that had taken Dominic away? She wanted it to disappear.

Dominic was throwing on some clothes, looking at her. "I think I'd better talk to whoever's out there, don't you?"

She said some words of agreement. "But hurry back."

"You know I will. I'd better cover you up, just in case someone peeks in. And let's hide the cuffs." She lowered her arms so the sheet he was smoothing over her covered it all.

After he'd walked away, she heard the voices more clearly. Pete was one of the people out there. In the dim light of the cabin, she could see Dominic wedged in the doorway after he'd opened the door the smallest amount necessary for him to take care of whoever was on the other side. She smiled to herself at the thought of his having to hide his very obvious erection from Pete and whomever he was with. Gwyn couldn't hear clearly what the people in the hallway were saying. Pete must have expressed concern that he couldn't find her, because she heard Dominic tell him she was there, in the cabin. Pete voiced surprise, his voice rising in annoyance or anger, becoming loud enough for Gwyn to hear clearly now.

"Yes, well, she's still not feeling ready to return to the party," Dominic said.

Pete, quite loud by now, said, "There goes the costume contest. I guess I'll have to take her home then."

Now Gwyn was surprised. Pete sounded almost like a grown-up, responsible adult. Of course, he gave greater priority to the costume contest than her needs—so what else was new?

"Not to worry, Payne. As soon as Ms. Verde is ready, I'll see that she gets home safely."

"Let me talk to her," Pete said, sounding as if he were moving closer to where she lay. Gwyn huddled tighter under the sheet. Pete continued, "Knowing her, she might get weirded out about me just leaving her here."

Great time to think of that, she thought, remembering how abandoned she'd felt earlier when he'd deserted her to speak with his buddies.

"I'll make sure she knows of your concern," Dominic said. "Now why don't you go back to the party? I'll join you shortly and leave Ms. Verde here to rest."

Next thing she knew, Pete was yelling her name. "Gwyn! Are you all right?"

She had no choice but to answer. "I'm resting. Mr. Laredo gave me an aspirin."

"You want to go home?"

She couldn't believe his concern coming now. "Mr. Laredo said his driver will take me home later. You can leave whenever you want."

"What about the costume contest?" Pete shouted back.

The costume contest again, of course. "Sorry, Pete. No can do."

She heard Pete grunt and make some more noise. Dominic said something to him. "Call me when you get home," Pete shouted. Then Gwyn heard more talking and, finally, the door closing.

When Dominic came back, he sat down next to her on the bed.

"Did you hear all that?" he asked.

"Most of it. So Pete finally remembered he had a date. Maybe all the other lost boys went back to their girlfriends."

Dominic ran an appreciative hand down her side, raising the most delicious shivers wherever his fingers landed. "Much as I would prefer to crawl back into bed and finish what we started, seeing Pete reminds me that I need to get back to the party for a bit. I did promise I'd give out awards for those best costumes."

She didn't want him to leave. Oh, she really didn't want to lose a single minute of their time together alone. But she was hardly in a position to make any demands. She pouted. "Hurry back."

"I will," he said, his eyes gleaming in the semi-darkness around them. "And," he said, his voice low and hoarse, "I'll give you my own personal best of show award later."

"Pete's pissed about losing," she said.

"In more ways than one." He smoothed his hair and finished reassembling his costume. "I'll be back as soon as possible," he promised.

Gwyn called him back. "The cuffs," she said, holding her hands out to him.

He chuckled. "Of course." He unlocked them and freed her hands, kissing each one tenderly, then left.

\*　\*　\*　\*　\*

When Dominic got back to the party, people were still eating and drinking, talking. He made a point of circulating, chatting with lots of his guests, checking out the costumes so he could select the prize winners. When he'd found the best for each category, he signaled to his assistant that the time had come to announce the winners. A drumroll and appropriate fanfare. Since Dominic's prizes included bottles of rare vintage wine, gourmet dinners delivered anywhere, and first-class transportation to the destinations of the winner's choice, the competition was lively. But Dominic's head wasn't there. He had to struggle to focus on his immediate task—and not on the woman waiting for him back in his quarters. Once he awarded the prizes, he'd be free to take leave of these festivities and return to the much more stimulating ones he was sharing with Gwyn.

The prize ceremony went well, if a trifle long. But finally, he could leave. Dominic could scarce hold back his giant relief and satisfaction. Something deep in him resonated with Gwyn Verde, left him confident and assured that she was the woman with whom he could build his dreams of the future. The quivering in his aching balls was a tangible reminder of how they'd been interrupted, and all that waited for him—for both of them.

She was so beautiful, so fresh and original. He'd never met anyone like her. She took his breath away with how she moved and what she said. And the way she responded to him. The way she was drawn to his special collection, her curiosity about all the things he wanted to explore. They were just at the beginning. He had so much more to show her, to learn from her. He just had to get through this damn party first.

# Hook, Wine & Tinker

\* \* \* \* \*

Good thing she'd remembered to have him remove her cuffs. Gwyn had limited tolerance for lying in bed alone while she waited for her lover to return. As if. Calling Dominic Laredo her lover didn't make it so. She knew that no matter how special and unique tonight felt, this would be a one-night stand. She certainly wasn't going to be fool enough to read any more into it than that.

Dominic had left the cuffs open on the night table. Now she picked them up and ran her fingers over the cooling metal. She wondered idly about the past uses Dominic had put them to. One thing she could be sure of, Dominic hadn't lived like a monk, just waiting for her. And he was too smooth to be a novice at using the cuffs or bringing a woman to a shuddering orgasm.

Did she have the nerve to explore his quarters by herself? Gwyn debated with herself for about two seconds before realizing she did. After all, hadn't he invited her to make herself at home? And just for tonight, wasn't she different than the rest of the time. Her usual rules of behavior were suspended, dangling somewhere over the Pacific. The first cabinet, the one where he kept the hook and the cuffs and what looked like other sets of cuffs, didn't seem to be locked. Her eye had caught so many different items she was curious about before. And then there was the other whole cabinet he hadn't even opened...

Acutely aware of her nudity, she slipped out of bed. She did not want to put the Tinkerbell outfit on again, but was way too warm to drape herself in her black silk cape. She never just walked around naked at home, and certainly hadn't when she was growing up in Aunt Nora's house. But here, being naked seemed totally reasonable.

Walking in the buff felt...great, natural. Like she was a woman of power, free, unfettered.

Bucking up her resolve, she opened the cabinet "her" cuffs had been in. The door moved smoothly when she tugged lightly on the porcelain knob. The metal hook was back in its place. Gwyn saw the empty spot her cuffs had been hanging on. Should she put them back? Would Dominic resent her entering his domain? From what she could see, Dominic appeared to like having his things placed precisely and methodically.

Dominic had lots of sets of cuffs—some similar to the ones she'd worn, others that looked more suitable for legs than arms. From the shining condition of each set, she could see he took very good care of his things.

She picked up a set of the leg irons and ran her fingers along their edges, careful not to smudge the gleaming metal. She wondered what it would feel like to make love with her ankles secured, her legs spread wide, her arms bound. And then she pictured Dominic attached to his bed with his own irons while she rode his amazing erection, moving all the ways she needed and wanted to... The heat in the pit of her stomach caused her clit to throb with need and hunger, made her wish he were here right now with her, so she could try out these poses with him. On second thought, a wave of shyness flashed through her—and she wondered if she'd really have the *cojones* to try. Then she laughed. Dominic certainly had awesome *cojones*—probably more than enough for both of them.

She put the leg irons back, planning how she'd surprise him when she whispered her desires to him later in the dark. She closed the door without having replaced "her" cuffs. Maybe they'd be put to use again tonight.

Gwyn couldn't stop wondering what Dominic kept hidden in his other cabinet. She licked her lips in anticipation. Did the second cabinet house even more exotic implements and toys than the first? Or maybe all it contained were his regular business clothes. Would that be a hoot? But why would he keep his wardrobe hidden away? The curiosity was killing her.

Gwyn reached for the porcelain knobs—and found these doors were much harder to open. After tugging for several seconds, she realized whatever Dominic kept here was probably far too personal for her to know about yet, hence the locks. Which made her all the hungrier to find out. What secrets could he have hidden away there? She already felt she'd learned so much about him. What deep, dark secrets did he choose to keep locked away from prying eyes—like hers?

\* \* \* \* \*

Dominic doffed his captain's tricorne and grinned wickedly as he watched Gwyn wrestle with his cabinet door. Each time she gave it a good tug, her delicious ass bounced with her effort, resonating in his cock—immediately rock hard for her. He once again locked his cabin door.

Voyeurism having its distinct limits, Dominic chose to announce his presence before Gwyn figured out how to open the cabinet doors herself. "Would you like to see what's in there?" he murmured softly.

Gwyn, clearly surprised that he'd come back, gasped, let go of the knobs, and flew backward to the bed—where she fell back, her legs forming a sensuous V. She sat up and sputtered, "You snuck up on me."

He shrugged lazily, stifling a chuckle. "I made as much noise as I could. But you were very focused on your task."

"Busted," she said. Then she blushed. "I'm sorry, Dominic. I didn't mean to intrude."

Still struggling not to laugh, he strode over to the bed and sat down next to her. "I have to admit I'd be disappointed if you weren't at least a little curious…"

"Then I guess you're not going to be disappointed," she admitted. "I'm more than a little curious…"

He cupped her lovely chin in his hand and looked deep in her eyes. "And your curiosity will be satisfied. Along with all your other needs. But, first things first. We left some unfinished business," he said, drawing her to him.

\* \* \* \* \*

She held herself back from his embrace for a moment, though she didn't want to. Once she melted into his arms, she knew all thought processes would come to a screeching halt. And she needed some information. "Is the costume party over?"

He raised an eyebrow. "As far as I'm concerned, the one out there is. But the one in here is just starting."

"Has Pete gone home?" she asked, wanting to see if she really was on her own with him now.

Dominic shrugged. "If he hasn't, he will soon. I've awarded the prizes. And I again assured him I'd see you safely home."

"Was he okay with that?" Gwyn asked, not altogether sure how she felt about Pete's easy acceptance of another man taking her home.

Dominic nodded. "He didn't ask many more questions. Such as exactly *when* I'd see you home." He drew her to him, and this time she didn't resist. "Too much talking," he whispered.

Finally, Dominic took her lips in a kiss that started gently and deepened in intensity in just moments, and any last resistance she felt dissipated. He stroked her face with his fingertips as his tongue probed deep into her eager mouth.

Now she wanted things to move more quickly. She pulled back from him and looked him up and down. "Too many clothes," she said. "You're wearing far too many clothes. Get naked like me."

"Of course," he said. "Help me." Licking her lips, Gwyn put her hands to work. Dominic had an amazing number of devices closing his costume. Eagerly, she unbuttoned and unhooked and unzipped, her fingers brushing his. As she worked, she stole glances at him, admired his powerful body as he revealed more and more of it to her. Dominic had the hard body of an athlete—not what she'd have imagined for a billionaire entrepreneur with a desk job. When they'd both managed to get him out of his black silk boxers, he stood before her for a moment, displaying his throbbing erection, which was finally set to find its intended and desired target.

\*  \*  \*  \*  \*

She looked at him from under hooded lids, and he could feel her preparing to welcome him into her. "I want you here. In the bed. With me. Now."

As he wanted exactly what she demanded, he stretched himself out next to her and took her in his arms. For this time, no cuffs, no irons, no toys. Just him and her. They could play with the toys more later, but for now, he wanted it to be just the two of them.

He nuzzled her neck and nearly jumped out of the bed when she grabbed his cock and began to stroke him.

He knew he couldn't hold out too long, and for this time, he didn't want to come in her hand.

"Foreplay," he moaned. "You keep doing that, and there won't be any."

"We already had foreplay," she said, her voice husky and the musk of her desire scenting the air. "I want you now, deep inside me."

He rolled onto her, wedging his thigh between her legs. Panting now, she began to ride his thigh, drenching his tight muscles with her hot moisture. He savored the wetness of her cunt, which reached to him with a welcome of heart-hammering proportion. He wanted to be in her so much, he gritted his teeth to keep from screaming. With his last shred of discipline, he reached for a foil packet in the drawer of his night table and drew out a condom.

She was wriggling, twitching with her need. "I want you, Dominic," she hissed, clutching his ass with fingers of steel.

He swallowed hard, then held up the condom. "Do you want me to put it on, or do you want to?"

"You," she moaned. "You put it on. Hurry." She sped up her ride, tightening her thighs around his.

He lifted himself from her taut embrace and fit the condom over his straining shaft. Then, shuddering on the verge of explosion, he positioned the tip of his penis at the mouth of her pussy and willed himself to move into her slowly. He wouldn't come before she did. He wouldn't come before she did... She wrapped her legs around him and pulled him to her. He thrust himself deep into her and she moaned his name, running her hands up and down his back.

"Dominic," she groaned, stretching his name to five syllables.

Nearly reeling with pleasure, he forced himself to move slowly and deliberately in her.

She bucked up her hips to meet him, pulling him into her tighter. He kissed her beautiful face, the moisture of his tongue sizzling at the contact with her hot skin.

Her hands gripped his ass, her fingernails digging into him. She sped up her dance, taking in his length faster, harder, deeper. "Let's slow this down," he whispered.

"Let's not," she whispered back, nipping his lips with her teeth.

He quivered at the edge of his release, wanting to let go and yet determined to bring her to her pleasure before he would take the plunge to his own satisfaction.

As her movements and her breathing accelerated, Dominic knew she was beginning to come. This was too much for him to bear. He knew he was going to explode into her like a firecracker. "There," she moaned when he'd caressed the most special place deep in her. "Oh, there.

Like that. Dominic, ahh..." She screamed his name as the pulses of her come pulled him deeper and tighter into her dark core.

And then he knew he couldn't wait a moment longer. An orgasm so deep and oh-so-necessary rocked him to his very essence. His pent-up semen flew out as if he'd been waiting for years to finally get laid. He came and came and came, emptying himself completely into her.

Drained and shaking from the power of his climax, he collapsed onto her in a sweaty, exhausted heap. "Gwyn," he sighed when he'd regained the power of speech. "Oh, Gwyn. Stay here with me. Be here with me." Usually he found the moments after orgasm the loneliest, but not with her.

She kissed him. "I'm here," she said. "I'm here now."

Sure he had to be crushing her with his weight, he carefully rolled off her, making sure he kept the condom in place. Lying next to her, he slowly pulled it off and tossed it into the wastebasket on the side of the bed. Then he took a handkerchief of black silk from his night table and wiped the love juices from her, then from himself.

"Oh God, Dominic. That was so amazing," Gwyn murmured, "I'm almost ready to start again."

"Give me a minute," Dominic said nuzzling her, knowing it wouldn't take much at all to get him hard again. He wondered if he'd ever be able to get enough of this beautiful, passionate woman.

\* \* \* \* \*

Nature, so to speak, called. Gwyn slipped out of bed to use the bathroom. Did they call it a head on a yacht, she wondered. Then she chuckled to herself thinking about when Dominic had given her head. She didn't want to stay out of the bed too long. She wanted every possible moment with this man this night. Not to mention that she fully intended to see what he kept in that second cabinet before his ship sailed out of her life.

But when she stepped into his bathroom, Gwyn caught her breath. This was no simple utilitarian facility. Dominic had created an ornate luxurious room, which included a state-of-the-art bidet and a huge antique footed tub. After she'd relieved herself and used the bidet, Gwyn ran her fingers over the tub, its golden knobs. Suddenly she wanted to take a bath here—to soak in the white porcelain expanse with Dominic's arms around her. She could picture them both submerged deep in the bubbles, washing each other's bodies and getting acquainted with all the hidden nooks and crannies...

When Gwyn came back out of the bathroom, Dominic was stretched out in the bed, his nude body spread eagle on top of the sheets. Even now, his cock rose in a semi-arousal she suspected would be very easy to advance to full bloom. But first, she really wanted to experience a luxurious bath with him.

"Where've you been?" he asked lazily.

"Checking out your amazing tub," she said, slipping onto the bed next to him. "You could fit three of my tubs in it." She thought for a moment. "Dominic, I'd sure like to take a bath in it. Would that be okay?" She wanted more than that, but she'd start by saying what she wanted for herself. With any luck, he'd join her. Or maybe she'd have to continue asking for what she wanted.

"A bath? Sounds great." He got out of the bed. "Ever have anyone draw a bath for you, fair Tinkerbell?" he asked, half bowing.

She pondered for a moment. "I don't think I have. Thank you, kind Captain Hook," she said.

He raised an eyebrow. "*Kind* Captain Hook?" he asked, sounding blustery. "Let's not let that get around."

"It's our secret," she whispered.

He cleared his throat. "While I'm getting the water just right, why don't you look in the cabinet under the sink? I have some bubble stuff and soaps. Select whatever you want."

"Okay."

She went back to the bathroom and opened the cabinet door. Saying he had *some bubble stuff and soaps* was as big an understatement as saying they were on a simple boat. When she took in all he had, Gwyn's eyes opened in surprise, though she should already have known Dominic would cover all bases. She'd seen bath stores with less varied and interesting inventory. For a brief moment, she wondered at the changing population of females who'd inspired Dominic to have all this stuff available—for surely the soaps and bubble baths, the skin gels and shampoos in all flavors of fruit and flowers, were not there for the use of this masculine man.

But Gwyn knew she had no right to question him about who the intended users were. After all, she'd come to Dominic's party with another man—and he was certainly not the first in her life.

Biting back her curiosity, Gwyn decided on lavender bubbles. Yummy as the scent was, she didn't think it was too feminine for a bath she hoped to share with Dominic. Anyway, he'd invited her to choose whatever she wanted.

Dominic was standing by the tub when she went over to it. The water—just hot enough and inviting—was streaming into the tub. "Found something you like?" he asked.

Gwyn handed him the bottle of bubble bath and a circle of hand-milled French lavender soap. He sniffed appreciatively. "I'd better put my hair up again," she said.

"There are some clips and pins in that cabinet."

Talk about equipped. Was there anything this guy didn't have at his fingertips? He went to the cabinet and came back with the a handful of clips that would do the trick. "Want me to help you?" he asked.

She nodded and turned her back to him. Within moments he'd deftly put up her hair, his hands strong and competent. She chuckled to herself thinking he'd have been a great hairdresser, wondered what he'd think if she said so. And then her thought processes disintegrated when he kissed the back of her neck. The water flowed into the tub soothingly, sending up wispy streamers of warmth.

Dominic rose, though she wished he'd stay where he was—even if the tub overflowed. "About that bath. Why don't you get the bubbles going? I've got towels warming," he said, indicating thick white terry draped over a large heating rack. "I need to get something else. I'll be right back."

Gwyn, wondering what in the world he'd be bringing back with him, watched him go. His butt reminded her of some statue she'd seen in an art book. One of the mythic heroes in Rome or Athens or one of the other places she'd always dreamed of going to.

Dominic returned quickly with a tray containing a bottle of champagne, two flutes, a platter of large fat strawberries, and dark elegant chocolates. "I realized you never got dessert—or much of anything else to eat," he said. "You must be starving."

She grinned. "Nothing that chocolate—and you—can't take care of."

He kissed her, then poured them each some champagne. He proposed a toast. "To J.M. Barrie," Dominic said, clinking his glass against hers.

She laughed, then took a great swallow of the champagne—which was delicious and went straight to her head. "I'm going to get into the tub," she said. She put her flute down on the tray and climbed in. She wriggled her bottom, getting comfortable in the deep tub, then turned the water off.

To her relief, he climbed in right behind her, filling the tub with his presence. "Is this acceptable?" he asked.

She nodded, closing her eyes and purring. The water was perfect, the bubbles fragrant, and she relaxed into the comfort of being there. Dominic leaned back against the edge of the tub, pulling Gwyn into the vee of his legs. She eased into the space he opened up for her, enjoying the feel of the bubbles popping and fizzing around them.

Speaking of bubbles, she reached over for the flutes, handed him his, and then took her own. They both sipped. She loved how the champagne softened her nerve endings, making her feel like the world was filled with bubbles—in her, around her, floating her in dreamy waves.

"Have you ever taken a bite of strawberry, a bite of chocolate, and then sipped champagne—all while you're sitting in a tub with a pirate?" Dominic asked.

"Everything but the last part," she said.

"Really?"

"No. Can't say I've ever done anything quite like this," she said, giggling.

"One of the pleasures of life not to be missed," he intoned seriously.

"Then I'll have to give it a try. I'm already in the tub with the pirate. So what first, the strawberry or the chocolate?"

He furrowed his brow. "From my vast experience with things hard and soft, I'd say the chocolate first. As you roll the hard chocolate around your tongue, you can add the soft strawberry—which melts in your mouth much faster. Then take a small sip of the champagne—and voilà! Complete ecstasy for your taste buds."

She had to stop laughing long enough to try his recipe. She bit into the chocolate, which was so dark and rich, she couldn't imagine anything else could add to its deliciousness. But he insisted that she take a nibble of the strawberry. Mmmm. "And now the champagne," he said.

He brought the flute to her lips and she took a small sip. The champagne fizzing over the chocolate and strawberry flooded her mouth with delight. When she'd swallowed and was about to thank Dominic for his suggestion, he turned her face to him and stopped her words with a kiss. His mouth was delicious with the snack they'd both shared, and he went to her head faster and more completely than any champagne.

When they broke apart, they just sat, their faces touching. "Do you know one of the top ten fantasies at my resorts involves making love in a bathtub?" he asked after a bit.

"Sounds like a bit of a logistical nightmare," she said thinking of her tub at home.

"Not in this tub, and there are even bigger ones at the resorts," he said. "Want to try it?"

"Uh, won't we splash all the water onto the floor?" She couldn't believe her inner housewife was coming out at this moment.

"Are you really worried about that?" he asked, grinning at her.

She laughed dryly. "Not really."

He kissed her. "Good. Anyway, the built-in drains will take any splashed water straight to the ocean below."

She waved her hand in an expansive gesture. "Sounds like you've thought of everything."

He toasted her. "That's the goal."

She toasted him back. "In that case, let's go for it."

He put his hands under her butt. "First we need to turn you around."

"Okay," she said. She leaned forward and got to her knees. Dominic ran his hand down the crack of her ass. "Hey," she protested. "What are you doing?"

"Just helping you to scrub everywhere," he said.

She turned around to face him and took advantage of the moment to splash him. "I can scrub myself there," she said.

"But it's so much more fun when I do it," he leered, twirling a mock mustache.

He was right. It was much more fun. But she wasn't going to admit that right now. "Okay, I'm turned around. Now what."

"Now you open those gorgeous legs and put them around my hips."

"You mean like this," she said, surrounding him with her legs, which caused a tidal wave of water to slosh out of the tub and left her sitting on his erection.

"Oh, yeah," he said, getting into it and her.

"Mmm," she said, as she began to rub herself against his growing cock. Who'd ever have believed she'd be ready again to make love so soon after she'd been so satisfied? Come to think of it, she'd so rarely been really satisfied, how was she to know how she'd feel afterward?

Dominic's head was burrowed between her breasts. He circled her left breast with kisses and love nips, his lips coming ever closer to her nipple, now standing at attention as he showered it with his special touches. Gwyn longed to press herself ever closer to this beautiful man who made her body sing. With each move, more of the bubbly water around them splashed out of the tub, expanding their watery world.

Dominic turned to her right breast, suckling with gusto. Pleasure coursed through Gwyn. She pressed her belly against Dominic's. She wanted him in her. Getting to her knees, she was able to angle herself so that she could slide down Dominic's throbbing shaft. He filled her with his warmth and hardness, taking her breath away with the sheer pleasure of his being there with her.

"Gwyn," he groaned out her name, and she met his mouth with hers.

His hands now on the cheeks of her ass, he moved her up and down along his thick, hard length. He moved a bit to the right, increasing the contact between his cock and her clit. She shuddered with the pleasure of his movements in her. As they moved together, the water continued to splash. The agitated waves amplified the sounds of their bodies colliding in a rhythm that quickly had them both gasping.

"Stop," Dominic said, holding her stationary with insistent hands, his fingers clutching her tush for dear life.

Not her first choice at the moment, but she willed herself to stay still for a moment. He lay buried so deep inside her. She wanted to move, but she also wanted him to stay where he was. With him in her, she felt safe and cared for in a way she never had before. It was as if this man knew everything about her, but he remained a mystery to her. "What is it?" she asked.

He exhaled. "I don't want to come yet."

She nibbled on his ear. "When can I start moving again?"

"How about January or February?"

She clenched the muscles of her dripping pussy around his cock, eliciting a huge groan from him.

He shifted his hips, and now his cock moved from side to side within her. She took that as a signal to resume her own movements. The muscle clenching and relaxing felt so good, she decided to continue for a bit. And then the small movement began to feel better and better. Before she knew it, Gwyn was climbing to her climax. Now she grasped his cock and moved, each tiny change of position bringing her higher and higher to her pleasure. And then she was there, coming, coming.

# Hook, Wine & Tinker

With a shout, Dominic withdrew his cock from her and began his own come—outside her, in the water. Gwyn watched, excited, as he spasmed and ejaculated. And then they collapsed together, suddenly finding their arms and legs entangled uncomfortably.

They managed to separate their limbs, and both stretched out in the tub, their heads leaning against the back. Dominic took Gwyn in his arms, and they entwined their legs again in a more comfortable position. "So what do you think about making love in a tub?" he asked.

Gwyn looked deeply at him and shrugged. "First impressions can be so misleading. I think I need to try it again, maybe fifty or a hundred times before I can be sure."

He laughed and then held her to him. "You're quite a woman, Gwyn Verde. Where have you been hiding all my life?"

Not knowing how to respond, she nuzzled him. They lay together for several minutes, savoring the warmth they'd generated and the comfort of the water.

"Now about that bath," Gwyn said, starting to sit up.

"Oh, right. How about if I soap you and you soap me?" Dominic asked, following her lead. He took the bar of soap and lathered up.

"We might never get out of the tub," Gwyn said as he gently washed the folds of her pussy.

"We'll grow fins and be entered in the *Guinness Book of Records*."

"We'll turn into two waterlogged prunes."

"Happy prunes," he said. "But we do need to exit from the tub. Other venues await and call." He gently planted a kiss on the top of her head, climbed out dripping water everywhere, and went to the heating rack to get them both towels.

He tied one around his middle, then came back to help her out of the tub. As soon as she'd set foot on the floor, he surrounded her with the warm comfort of a perfectly heated towel and began gently rubbing her dry. She loved the feel of the towel almost as much as she loved the feel of his hands on her.

"Do you want to leave your hair up?" he asked, massaging her neck.

She shook her head. "No, will you take it down for me?"

He grinned and thrust his fingers into her hair, lightly rubbing her scalp after he'd removed the pins.

"That was the best bath I've ever had in my life," she said. "But now, I don't have any clothes to put on."

He looked at her in surprise. "What about your Tinkerbell costume?"

"Oh, that," she said, waving her hand dismissively. "That was Pete's idea, his costume for me. It's just a cheap bit of junk."

"You deserve far better than a cheap bit of junk," he said. "Let's see if we can find you something more suitable—for when you get dressed. Because for right now, what you're wearing is fine."

"You mean the towel?"

"I mean the birthday suit." He eyed her very appreciatively.

When they'd each helped towel the other off, they went back out to the bedroom. "So where do you have other clothes I can wear?" Gwyn asked, looking around.

"Later. I promise later I'll show you, and you'll have lots of time. But for now, why don't you tell me your favorite fantasy?"

She laughed. "My favorite fantasy?" She laughed, then shook her head. "Dominic, this whole night has been better than any fantasy I've ever come up with. Why don't you tell me yours."

"You're sure?" he asked, looking a bit disappointed. "No other fantasy you can think of?"

"Honest, I'm all out of fantasies. But I'd really love to hear what you dream of."

He put his arms around her and sat her down on the bed. He looked deep in her eyes. "Gwyn, I will tell you my favorite fantasy on one condition."

"Sounds ominous," she said. "What? You think your fantasy will have me running out of here, kicking and screaming?"

He laughed dryly. "I hope not. Gwyn, I'll tell you what I want on one condition." He ran his fingertips over her face in a way that gave her goose bumps. "I'm going to describe something I'd love to do with you."

"Okay, Dominic," she said. "I'm all ears." She closed her eyes.

"Please look at me," he said.

She opened her eyes.

"I want you to promise that you'll agree to do it only if you really want to." His eyes were dancing as he watched her.

"Okay," she said.

"I don't want to do *anything* that will hurt you or scare you or make you feel less than thrilled with me."

What could he possibly be talking about? She scowled. "You're really scaring me with what you're saying," she said, now feeling far too naked and vulnerable to him and wishing she had something reasonable to cover herself with.

"Sorry for sounding so ominous. I'd better just tell you what it is." He got up and went to the cabinet he'd opened before. He opened the door and took out...the leg irons she'd been touching before. "We made love with your hands cuffed together. I'd like to go one step further...and love you with your legs cuffed down and your hands attached to the headboard."

He put the cuffs down and went back to her. He sat down next to her and began to stroke her arms.

That was all? After his big build-up, she hadn't known what to imagine he had in mind. Heck, his ideas were pretty close to her own. She suddenly felt shy about telling him her earlier fantasies—including that he be the one who was cuffed. But, oh, she wanted him. Even more now. She wanted to live out his fantasies...and hers.

But was it politic to admit all that? Remnants of the lessons and strategies she'd always used in her relationships with men floated to her consciousness.

She looked at Dominic and at the irons he'd left on the bedside table and licked her lips.

# Chapter Four

Gwyn looked from the irons to Dominic and back. He was watching her so intently, waiting to hear what she'd say. Maybe she'd tell him he could make love to her using the leg irons on her only if she got the chance to use them on him first. The image of this powerful man helpless to move except in the ways she ordered got her juices flowing and her clit vibrating in expectation. They were sitting in his bed. The sheets felt surprising cool to her butt after all the heat they'd generated together just a short time before. Now she could easily imagine them generating lots more heat together soon. Heck, if they were going to start filling each other's deepest fantasies, maybe they'd just scratched the surface of how good they could be together. Suddenly she felt that whatever there was between them had entered a whole other dimension and depth.

But before she opened herself up to filling his fantasies and really let him into her own, she wanted to know what made him tick. She had no doubt that tonight he could have been with most—if not all—of the women at the party and huge numbers of women from the rest of the world. Why had he picked *her* out—and she was sure he'd done exactly that. Was it just the costume going along so well with his, or was there something else going on that she didn't know about yet?

She reached out and touched the implements in his hands. "Why do you want to use these on me?" she asked.

She suspected the irons simply turned him on as much as they did her—but she wanted to know the next level of what was going on with him.

He looked thoughtful. "Would it convince you to go for them if I told you they're part of my Captain Hook fantasy—especially with Tinkerbell, a fairy who could use her magic to escape me?"

She shook her head. "Not enough." Being Tinkerbell had been a fluke, not at all the costume she would have picked. If the Captain Hook-Tinkerbell thing really was his major motivation, she'd be so disappointed. It would cast a pall on what would surely be one of the most memorable nights in her life. Well, a slight pall. Bedazzled as she was at this moment, she knew there wasn't much that could mess up what they had now. Nonetheless, she persisted in digging. "You mean anybody who showed up in a Tinkerbell costume tonight would have done for you? What if there had been two of us wearing the same costume?"

He waggled his eyebrows at her. "An interesting prospect," he said, grinning wolfishly. "Two Tinkerbells. Kind of boggles the mind with possibilities."

She frowned, not pleased he was taking her question so lightly. He reached out and stroked her face gently with his fingertips. "If there had been two Tinkerbells tonight," he said hoarsely, "I'd have had no problem picking which one this Captain Hook wanted in his bed and in his irons. Oh, Gwyn, it's you. I don't know if I can tell you everything I'm thinking without really scaring you. But I've waited so long for a woman like you. No, for *you*. And you've come to me in a costume matching my role for the party. Ever hear of synchronicity?"

Maybe somewhere, vaguely. "What is synchronicity?" she asked, fastening on the easiest part of what he'd said in response to her first question.

He looked thoughtful. "A wonderful way the universe has of bringing the right people together at just the right time."

"You mean coincidence?" she asked. This guy sounded more like some guru than a billionaire entrepreneur.

"Nothing that mundane." He stroked her arm in almost hypnotic fashion. "Look. No matter why you're wearing this costume, no matter what means fate or destiny or kismet or whatever used, the important thing is you are here. With me."

Enthralled by the sound of his voice and the feel of his fingers, Gwyn nonetheless pulled back. Whoa. This guy was throwing around some big heavy words—fate, kismet, synchronicity—that she had not at all expected in response to her lighthearted question. He seemed so keyed into her. He pulled back at the same time, as if realizing his intensity might scare her shitless.

"So what costume would you have worn if you'd had your druthers?" he asked.

Interesting question. What would she have picked? Dominic was challenging her to put her money where her mouth was, and for once, she didn't know what to say. He was watching closely, apparently avid to hear her response.

Her brain had started turning to mush several orgasms ago, not to mention how good it felt as he kept so lightly stroking her arms, her face. His touch was like butterfly wings on a flower petal as he absorbed the planes of her face with his fingertips. That plus the champagne she'd consumed, and the food she hadn't, seemed to short-circuit her thought processes. "Cleopatra," she said, glomming onto the first person who popped into her consciousness. "I'd have been Cleopatra."

He looked surprised. "A luscious blonde like you would hide under a brunette wig?"

She nodded, the idea growing on her.

"And who would I be?" he whispered. "Caesar? Marc Antony?"

"You," she said, "would be my humble slave. Fanning me with giant leaves." And then she mock swooned as he began to mock fan her.

"A slave is good for fanning with palm fronds and peeling grapes for the great queen," he said, stretching out next to her and speaking softly, "but who's going to service her? Surely no mere slave would suffice. A prince, a general. Tell me, Caesar or Antony?"

Gwyn pouted petulantly. "Princes and generals are all good in their proper place. But sometimes the Queen of the Nile desires diversity in her bedchamber." She leaned over and tongued his ear before whispering breathily, "Be my slave, Dominic. My love slave."

By now Dominic's throbbing erection signaled his eagerness to comply with Cleopatra's directives.

"My Queen, as you can see," he said sheepishly, indicating his risen mast, "you have convinced me to play the role you want in your fantasy. But tell me, Your Majesty, how does the queen's humble slave dress?"

Dominic's rapid capitulation to her wish scenario surprised and excited Gwyn. Though she'd just pulled the Cleopatra name and idea from her imagination, she now began to wonder how they could bring such role play to life. She looked over at his erection, licked her lips, and said, "We're in a hot climate. Very hot. Tropical desert. A slave needs to wear very little. Especially because his queen desires to feast her eyes and hands and lips freely on his jewels. A simpleloin cloth she can remove at will...that's all that's required." She frowned. "But of course the queen must have a much more elaborate wardrobe."

He rose from the bed. "How fortunate for the humble slave that he knows the way into the queen's secret wardrobe... Her oils and unguents, her special jewels and gowns. And of course, her famous wig. For you, the slave will bring the queen's special accoutrements and help her put them on. For there is no service this humble servant would ever deny his queen."

Being with Dominic led from surprise to surprise, an ongoing adventure though they'd never left his quarters. Gwyn sat up slightly from the pillows she was reclining against and watched Dominic go to the second cabinet, the one she hadn't been able to open earlier. He reached somewhere, came up with a tiny key, and opened the doors. Within moments he'd brought out a white sheet he wound around himself in loincloth fashion. He twirled around so she could see him from every angle.

She studied him critically. "I think that cloth needs to be tighter," she said.

"Where, Your Majesty?" he asked.

"Between your legs, slave," she said. "Your queen requires to be able to judge your state of, uh, readiness to serve at all moments."

*****

If he got much more ready to serve, he'd explode, he thought. Nonetheless, he tightened the white cotton—not to exactly tourniquet level, but so it left little to the imagination. Another runway twirl before her.

She watched critically. "That will do, slave."

Then he bowed to her in humble eastern fashion. Dominic could barely suppress his delight as he watched Gwyn watching him. She was so tuned into him, it was as if she had a window to his dreams and fantasies. Whereas before, he'd always felt he was leading the few women who penetrated this far into his private kingdom. Gwyn seemed to know what to say and do instinctually. In fact, sometimes it was like she was leading him. Things were moving fast, maybe too fast. Whatever he did, he had to make sure he didn't scare her away as he almost had with the leg irons before. But the way she was playing his game, he had the feeling his instincts would keep him as on track with her as she was with him. He hoped.

So she wanted him to be her slave? From the way she was constructing her fantasy, Dominic realized he'd probably be the one wearing leg irons and handcuffs before she was. But that was all right. He chuckled to himself, realizing he couldn't remember the last time he'd let anyone tie him down—in *any* way. But Gwyn wasn't like anyone else he'd ever let in his life before.

By letting her have her way, he could show he trusted her, be a model for when they did turnabout and he became the "master." Besides, it had been a long time since anyone had turned the tables on him and maneuvered him into being the one restrained. He had to admire Gwyn for the quick and easy way she'd come up with this strategy. His cock did a small jig in anticipation of what she'd come up with for him as his queen.

He bowed down to his queen, then moving backward so as not to offend her, he went over to the cabinet and took out the Cleopatra costume, heavy in its garment bag It had been a long time since this one was used. Heck, it had been a long time since any of them had been used. Too long.

Though he loved Gwyn's blond good looks, Dominic had to admit to a special fondness for the Cleopatra look. The costume included a short white silk gown with a simple drape, fourteen-carat gold bracelets and arm bands as well as a headband that went over the thick ebony wig, a magnificent necklace of turquoise and more gold, and heavy gold hoop earrings. Just as he'd told Gwyn, he had pots of creams and sweet scented perfumes. He wouldn't have wanted to vouch for their historical authenticity, but he could vouch for their sensual potential.

Gwyn watched him open-mouthed as he drew these items from his special cabinet. He smiled to himself, only too aware of the other costumes and props housed in this cabinet—and the uses he and Gwyn could put them to in the future.

"Your Majesty," he said, "please allow your slave to approach you."

She gestured regally for him to come forward.

"May your slave be permitted to anoint you with the secret sacred creams made just for you before we robe you in your garments and jewels?"

Though her eyes were wide with curiosity and questions, Gwyn appeared to want to enter fully into her role play. She indicated her acquiescence with a languorous wave of her hand. "Very well, slave. Come forward. Anoint your queen. But first, I need to don my headdress."

"Of course," he said, holding the heavy wig to her for her inspection. She tucked back her hair with her hands and held her head forward for him to slip the wig on.

When she had the wig and the hair ornament on, Dominic gasped despite himself. Most blondes did not make an easy transition to being brunettes. He'd been afraid she was too pale to carry off wearing the wig, but now he saw it made her look sultry and even sexier. She looked harshly at him, and he remembered his position. "What is it, slave?" she asked haughtily.

"May I hold up the mirror so Your Majesty can see if the head covering suits her?"

"Of course," she said.

He went over to the dresser and came back with an ornate silver mirror, which he held up to her.

She almost gasped when she saw herself, but then appeared to catch herself. She motioned her slave to put the mirror back.

When he returned, she asked, "Which cream have you prepared to use today for my massage?"

Dominic picked up a tray with two glass jars on it, one cobalt blue, the other amber. As with everything else, he'd had these custom made—and they were filled with creams made according to recipes he'd researched and improved upon. "I hesitate between milk and honey or rosewater, Your Majesty. What is my lady's pleasure?"

She furrowed her brow as if contemplating the weightiest of matters. "I think the rosewater today," she said at last.

"Your wish is my command." He bowed low and opened the blue jar,. The fragrance of roses spread over the room.

* * * * *

Now Gwyn lay back among the pillows and felt the thick black hair spread out beneath her. She'd have assumed that a wig would be uncomfortable, and was pleasantly surprised at how good this one felt on her head. After looking in the mirror, she knew how amazing she looked in the wig.

Her slave, who'd obviously been well trained in the art of massage among his other talents, began to work the rose-scented cream into her skin—starting with each toe. He slowly and methodically rubbed the cream into her thirsting skin as if he had infinite time to devote to each surface. With his skilled fingers, he seemed to focus on those nerve endings on a direct route to her clit. Come to think of it, all her nerve endings seemed wired to her clit. Stimulating and relaxing at the same time, his massage transported her like a slow boat trip down the Nile. When she finished her stint as queen, Gwyn would have to ask Dominic where he got this marvelous cream, which delighted her nose almost as much as it brought a glow to her skin. But then she banished the thought of later, which intruded the modern world and reality into her reverie.

Or maybe it was her slave's skilled and attentive touch that set her skin to singing. Maybe he could have been rubbing raw mud into her and producing the same results. Everywhere his fingers went, Gwyn began to experience new sensations and fresh awareness of her body. She truly began to feel like a queen, an empress at least as great as Cleopatra. Though she didn't want her slave to get too exalted an opinion of his skills, she allowed herself to moan her pleasure. Discreetly, of course. She'd have to find other means than suppressing her sounds of pleasure to keep him humble.

"Milady," he murmured softly, "may I have your permission to speak?"

Gwyn/Cleopatra almost chuckled at the prospect of this powerful man asking her if he could speak. Oh, she could definitely get used to this. She swallowed her laugh and, as haughtily as she could, waved her hand at him and said, "Yes, slave. As long as what you say does not displease me." It was a challenge to keep her tone imperial as he massaged the cream into the sensitive crease between her left thigh and her moist hungry pussy lips.

"With your permission. I was just thinking of the time I had the honor to massage Her Majesty as we floated on the royal barge down the Nile under a full moon," he said softly.

"Ah, yes," she said. His fantasy coincided with hers. Talk about synchronicity. Gwyn was almost beginning to believe it really existed. She longed to have the experience they'd both imagined. Floating down the Nile on a barge. The pyramids. Heck, she'd even enjoy paddling around San Diego Bay if Dominic was massaging her. Just being in the bathtub with him had been ecstasy.

Of course, she'd always dreamed of really traveling. That was why she chose to work in the travel industry. Egypt was high on her list of places to tour—and at least as far out of her reach as Greece and Rome and China and just about everywhere else, even with her professional discounts. Heck, at this point, she couldn't swing a few days in New York. But a girl could dream. Tonight felt exactly like she was dreaming. She pushed Gwyn out of the picture to revel in being Cleopatra and having a faithful, very talented slave to serve her. Tomorrow would come soon enough.

Her slave was continuing to speak softly, soothing words that had no real meaning, as he massaged the cream into the taut skin below her navel. His questing fingers skirted all around the welcoming folds of her cunt, increasing her desire to feel him there, raising that desire notch by delicious notch. She debated whether pressing her pussy into his hand would diminish her dignity. But he appeared to be asking something that required a response.

"Would you like me to arrange another barge ride for you? The full moon is once again near upon us," he said, his hands making slow lazy circles on her belly—alas, too far from her cunt for her to just arch and have his hand where she wanted it.

"Yes," she said sharply. "But attend to what you are doing now."

"Of course," he said, bowing his head.

When her slave had completed a most thorough massage, Gwyn/Cleopatra felt pampered, calm, and amazingly turned on. His eyes flashing, he asked, "Your lowly slave humbly requests to know, what next for Her Majesty's pleasure?"

Gwyn thought about the leg irons. But that wasn't the game right now. First she needed to get dressed in the Cleopatra clothes—even if she'd be undressing again within moments. "Your queen is ready to dress for the day," she said.

He brought the gorgeous garment and jewelry over to her. His dream woman must be just her size, as the short robe fit almost as if custom made for her. And the jewelry was like a treasure trove. Hard to believe it was all real, but of course it was. She already knew that Dominic wouldn't have it any other way. She carefully removed her diamond studs and put them in a little crystal dish. The Cleopatra earrings weighed her ear lobes down, bringing new sensitivity there.

"Would Your Majesty care to look in the large mirror?" the slave asked.

"Yes," she said.

He led her to the first cabinet and opened the door to a full-length mirror. Gwyn loved how she looked already, and thought about how having the right makeup for a brunette would really finish the look. What a contrast to the cheap Tinkerbell costume she'd put on earlier that night. "This will do," she told her slave in royal understatement.

Now that she was fully costumed, Gwyn's thoughts went back to those leg irons always lurking beneath the surface of her thoughts. Did she dare ask him to put them on? Did she dare use them with him? Her heart began to race at the prospect, and her clit began to twitch. Just seconds of visualizing Dominic her captive in the irons blasted holes in the serenity of a moment before.

She wanted to use them, but what if...? What if what? Her concern was maybe she'd somehow turn Dominic off, never see him again if he knew she desired to have her way with him attached to his bed.

As if. As if she was ever going to see him again. That thought was as big a fantasy as her being the Queen of the Nile. Dominic Laredo was a major player, and she'd just opportunistically come along in a costume that went with his on an off night. The only reason she'd been available to go with him was because her boyfriend had chosen to ignore her so he could spend time with his buddies. But she wasn't dazzled enough to think anything real or lasting could come out of the night's adventures. Dominic Laredo was so out of her league, she couldn't even believe they were having this one night together.

She held her regal, bejeweled head up high. She had nothing real to lose. Even if her fantasy totally turned him off, he'd go along — and then quietly send her off on her way. Or maybe he wouldn't even bother going along. He was a big boy. Besides, he probably wouldn't be completely turned off. After all, these were *his* toys she was playing with. So, what the hell? She'd go for it.

Swallowing hard, she looked at him and lowered her eyes almost flirtatiously, but maintaining her haughtiness. "You've done very well so far, slave," she said using the slow and measured speech she imagined Cleopatra would have. This woman really had had all the time and resources in the world. No need ever to rush or to analyze her impulses to death... "Now for your next task, you will fetch those irons and cuffs and bring them back to the royal bed." She sat down on that royal bed to wait.

His face a blank mask, he bowed his head slightly and said, "Very good, Your Majesty."

Licking her lips, Gwyn watched Dominic cross over to the nightstand where he'd previously left the cuffs for feet and hands. She loved seeing how his muscles rippled as he moved across the room in his loincloth, sleek and powerful as a panther she'd trained to respond to the sound of her voice. She suppressed a small giggle as she thought that maybe he'd left the implements there thinking he'd use them on her. Turnabout was such sweet play.

Dominic/Slave picked up each item, held it up for her inspection with great reverence, and brought the whole lot over to her. He held them out to her. "What is your wish, my Queen?" he asked.

She sighed delicately. If she seriously wanted him bound to the bed, she'd have to move her derrière from its very comfortable spot. Oh, the sacrifices royalty had to put up with. Her desire to get him on his back surpassed the comfort of sitting and watching, so she got up.

"Slave, now you will pleasure me in all that I say," she said.

"Of course," he said.

"You'll recline here on my bed when I tell you, slave," she said indicating where she wanted him.

"Milady, this humble servant requests only to please you," he said, bowing his head slightly but not before Gwyn caught the gleam in his eye and the slight smile lifting the corners of his scrumptious mouth. She could swear she saw him surreptitiously lick his lips.

Well she was a generous queen. Let her slave enjoy himself as she took her pleasure from him. "I will tell you what to do next." And next and next, she thought.

"I await your word with bated breath," he said.

Right, she thought. "First, remove your loincloth." He began to unwind the cloth at a leisurely place. Gwyn/Cleopatra was pleased to see his erection was not just a trick of the way the fabric was wound. "Faster." He complied. This was fun. She clamped her lips tight with suppressed laughter. It wouldn't do for her slave to see she was amused.

When he was totally nude, he stretched himself out on the bed and Gwyn feasted her eyes for a moment. What a magnificent specimen of male flesh. She'd enjoy herself enough with him tonight to last her the rest of her life.

He'd accommodatingly left the cuffs open so she could make easy work of fastening him to the bedposts.

"Spread out your hands and feet," she commanded. He obligingly went into a spread eagle pose that raised the rate of her heartbeat and nearly had her crossing her legs to keep her intimate moisture from overflowing its banks like the Nile bringing fecundity to the parched land.

She found it surprisingly easy to attach her slave to the convenient posts of the head and foot of the bed. When he lay there, totally exposed and vulnerable, arms and legs stretched and secured, a moment's doubt warred with her burgeoning desire. "Dominic," she asked, "is this really all right? Does it hurt to be cuffed?"

He looked at her in almost a disparaging way. "This miserable slave aspires only to please his queen. He does not matter, except as to how he serves. Has he done something to displease Her Majesty? If so, he apologizes from the bottom of his abject soul."

Gwyn blinked twice. Dominic was really holding true to his role in his play with her. Well if he was determined to maintain the fantasy, so would she.

\* \* \* \* \*

Dominic couldn't believe how fantastic it was to be with this woman. He'd nearly come just from massaging her with the rose cream. He wanted to lick every inch of her, to straddle her and pump his aching shaft and balls on her and in her. Up until she actually fastened him to his bed, he'd seriously doubted she'd have the nerve. Good for her. She'd surprised him yet again, which only added to his enjoyment of her. One thing he was already learning about Gwyn—never to underestimate her.

He'd nearly broken out of his slave role when he'd talked about taking a barge ride down the Nile with her in the moonlight. There was something about him and traveling on water. People who accused him of wanting to live full time on the Bound for Pleasure weren't far off the mark. Now that she'd come into his life, Dominic longed to travel the world by sea with her by his side. With Gwyn, he again wanted to see the places his jaded eyes had grown to take for granted, with her fresh excitement to reinspire him he'd once more be ready to conquer new worlds. Of course it wouldn't do for the slave to proffer such invitations to the exalted empress who was about to let him serve her, but later…

She was looking at him so intently, as if her eyes could pierce to the deepest corners of his soul. And then she began to fondle his straining erection, and he couldn't help but move—as much as his restraints let him, which wasn't much. She'd fastened him down quite effectively.

\* \* \* \* \*

Gwyn hiked up her imperial robe, removed her imperial undergarment, and straddled her gorgeous imperial slave. If he hadn't been so fantastic to touch, she might have been satisfied with just taking him in with her eyes, engraving his image onto her mind forever. But she couldn't keep her hands or her mouth or her other bodily parts off him. And as his queen, she didn't have to.

First she stretched herself along his well-muscled length, loving the feel of his rock hard erection pressed against her belly. She wanted to start with a long, lingering kiss, trying to convince herself that she had all the time in the world to do whatever she wanted with him. She stroked his face as her tongue began to probe the delicious depths of his waiting mouth. Despite the implied passivity of his pose, his tongue and lips were anything but passive as her kiss sparked a hot response from him. He may have been a slave, but his tongue was more than equal to hers—thrusting into her, demanding her surrender to him. She breathed him in, chewing on his full lips, his tongue. Their kiss deepened as each gave way to the growing hunger moving them.

She broke the kiss and lay her head on his chest, between his two erect nipples, brown against his golden tan. She listened to the fierce hammering of his heart, knowing his accelerated beat betrayed her power over him.

Gwyn ran her hands down his sides from his outspread armpits to his well-shaped ankles. Her slave, who was hard and firm everywhere, moaned, feeding her excitement. She longed to ride his huge cock, to move her hips in all the ways that would bring maximum pleasure to her, to both of them. But she wanted to extend their ecstasy, make this moment last 'til she could suck the last drop of it dry for her memories. He had a small brown mole right over his waist on the right side and an interesting bruise on his left hip. She touched the bruise and he winced. Later, she would ask him how he'd hurt himself.

But now she buried her head on his flat, firm belly, so close to his aroused penis. She licked the skin near his navel, tasting his salt and strength, enjoying the rippling of his muscles as he writhed beneath her. She was about to put her lips to his cock when she more fully realized what power she had over this man at this moment. Despite his enormous strength, she knew she could hurt him—in many ways. She could bite or kick or injure him, for he'd let her put him at her mercy. For now, he was truly as subject to her as the humble slave to Cleopatra. She blew softly on his cock and watched him move.

He lay there, so open to her. No, she'd never hurt him. But he'd had no way of knowing that for sure when he lay down and spread himself out for her. Her recognition of his trust and faith in her nearly knocked her off the bed, its impact greater than any of the other amazing revelations of the night. This man lay before her, completely hers to do with as she would. She bit back tears of amazement as she absorbed this truth. There'd be time for the tears later, much later. Now she would pleasure him as she took her own joy from him. Her pussy and clit were nearly as engorged as his turgid cock.

As she cupped his full, heavy balls in her hands, she ran the tip of her tongue slowly around the head of his penis. He writhed beneath her, gasping. "My Lady," he said, staying in role as she played with him. "I'm yours to do with as you will." Ah, yes. He was.

When she leaned into him, her necklace fell away from her neck, forming a jeweled curtain between his cock and his balls. The moment Gwyn realized this, she swung the necklace back and forth in a tiny motion that she repeated, soon adding little squeezes of his balls. Her slave's moans told her she was using her jewels most effectively. She giggled to herself, wondering if the designer had ever envisioned how the gold and precious stones could enhance a magnificent erect cock.

As much fun as she was having, she realized neither she nor her slave could continue without their play leading to the predictable end. Even a queen as powerful as Cleopatra couldn't stop nature. And she would have her wild ride before the last of this game. For just these few moments, she knew the magnificent slave pleasuring her would be totally hers.

She reached for a condom on the edge of the table and opened it quickly. Dominic, her slave, groaned when she unfurled it over his waiting staff. With a final pat to his balls, Gwyn lifted her hips and angled herself down to engulf her slave's prize tool. Once he'd penetrated her, she sat for just a moment, savoring the feel of him buried deep inside her.

"Now, my pet," she whispered, "you will take your queen on a most special ride. You are my champion stallion, and together we will jump the fences and race through the desert."

"Yes, Your Majesty," he whimpered. "As you wish."

She wished to start slowly, lifting her hips so high she nearly came to edge of his cock. Just before she would have slipped off the end, she slid back down. Too delicious. Each movement produced an echo of wetness and hardness meeting head on. She had to allow herself to release the sounds that would tell him he was pleasing her.

But she had to be careful. Her slave could not know how he was affecting her, or he might lead a palace insurrection. Then he arched his hips to move up to meet her downward slide, and she gave up any pretensions to dignity. So her slave would get a swelled head. To hell with revolutions. She bit back a laugh. She loved what happened when other parts of his anatomy swelled.

She stretched out full length along his torso and kissed his lips, first tenderly, then with more fervor, as her hips continued the up and down dance that took his shaft the length of her hot, tight sheath. She felt him grow yet larger and she began a circular rotation with her hips, first clockwise, then counter clockwise. He called out her name—"Cleopatra, my Queen!"

Gwyn put her hands on his butt, though there wasn't much room between his glorious ass and the bed. Damn, she'd really fastened him tight. His writhing and wriggling added to her pleasure, deepening her vibrations 'til she thought she'd scream. And she wasn't even coming yet, though she knew it would not be long.

"My love," he called out, "stop, or it won't be much longer 'til your slave..."

He'd called her his *love*. She knew it had to be the sex talking—she wouldn't fall into the trap of taking anything he said right now seriously. Nothing anyone said in the throes of... "Oh, God," she called out, rising to a new peak of pleasure.

Oh, yeah. It was happening now. She was climbing that slope and seeing stars and circles of blinding white light. She was floating in outer space, among the planets and the galaxies and the suns. She might never return to earth. She heard her voice scream out his name and unintelligible fragments of words as her mind and body exploded.

As her release shattered the air around them, he began to pulse with his own, pulling against his cuffs, calling her name, then sending gallons of his come into her quivering core. He said her name and the "L" word again, and the rest was too much for her fogged brain to begin to untangle.

The queen collapsed in a most unroyal heap on the drained body of her slave.

* * * * *

Dominic would never be able to get enough of her. Though he'd slipped into the role of slave to accommodate Gwyn in her Cleopatra role, he felt only too clearly that he could very easily become a love slave to this woman. She brought him to such heights of pleasure that after just a few hours together, he couldn't imagine having to be without her.

Now she lay on him, their hearts hammering together in harmony. His arms and legs were still cuffed, so he couldn't embrace her. For now, he would put up with this restraint, which was so unlike how he was in any other segment in his life. He shifted slightly, aware of Gwyn on top of him and the gentle movements of the waters far beneath them.

But then he couldn't stand the restraints a moment longer. He *had to* be free to touch her or he'd die. "Gwyn," he whispered to her, "release me."

She raised her face and looked at him. "So I'm no longer Cleopatra?" Her lips curved sardonically.

"For now," he said, "it's time to end this part of the story, Your Majesty." He chuckled dryly. "You see, I want to touch you, and I need my hands back for that."

"Oh," she said, moving slowly.

"And to be honest, I'm losing the circulation in several of my limbs."

"Oh, right," she said, moving more quickly and climbing off him. "Uh, Dominic, where are the keys?"

He explained exactly where everything was and how to release him. As soon as she'd freed him, both of them rubbed the feeling back into his ankles and wrists. Then he held her to him and satisfied his need to stroke her beautiful face. "Gorgeous as you look as a brunette, I'm ready for you to go back to being a blonde. Let's take off your wig so I can have Gwyn back."

She handed him the wig.

"And maybe it's time to retire Cleopatra for now. If you'll take off the costume, you can put this on." He handed her a beautiful jade green kimono that he'd gotten the last time he went to Japan.

"Okay," she said, looking a bit regretful. She quickly took off the costume and put on the kimono. "But can I keep some of the jewelry on?"

"If you want," he said, stroking her softly. He took the wig from her as she fluffed up her blond hair.

"Gwyn, tell me how that was for you," he asked.

"What do you mean?" she asked, turning from the mirror where she'd been frowning at her reflection.

He ran his fingers down her face, then kissed her lightly. "How was it for you having me as your slave, cuffed, while you, as they say, had your way with me?"

She appeared to close off from him, and he didn't understand why. He thought they'd gotten so intimate just before. "Fine. It was fine," she said. "How was it for you?" She looked a bit nervous to hear his response.

He took both of her hands in his. "God, Gwyn it was fucking fantastic." He shrugged at his inability to find the words he needed to tell her exactly what she meant to him, how it had been for him. He, Dominic Laredo, who was never at a loss for words or much of anything else. "You know," he added, groping to express himself, "I felt we were really into it, up on a whole new level of being together. I know I sound like some new age guru mouthing platitudes. But damn, I don't know how else to say it."

She sighed and said so softly he had to bend to catch her words, "I know this night is going to be one of the most special of my whole life."

Though the words themselves seemed positive, Dominic sensed a deep sadness in what she was saying—and in how she expressed herself—and that damnable holding back. Why, when they'd had such soul shattering sex and beyond, was she sounding *sad*? How could he ask her this when he intuited she'd begun to put a wall up between them and everything he was doing right now only had her piling the bricks higher?

\* \* \* \* \*

It was so funny, Gwyn thought. Pete often accused her of wanting to talk too much after sex, of wanting to analyze their lovemaking to death. She'd always been frustrated by his refusal to verbalize at all about their sex—let alone anything like feelings—except for an occasional grunt. But now *Dominic* was the one trying to generate some talk, trying to draw her out, and she was the one keeping silent. He wanted her to give him information she quickly realized she didn't want to share with him. Not now, maybe not ever. It wasn't at all that she didn't *feel* close to him, because she did. She amazed herself when she realized just how close she felt to him—closer than she ever had with any of her previous partners. But she also realized that what he thought about her mattered, a lot. Probably way more than it should. What would he think if she told him she knew this was a one-night stand, and the prospect of never seeing him again made the rest of her life stretch ahead like a long gray road to nowhere?

One thing she knew for sure. She didn't want to ruin this night by clinging. Dominic Laredo wasn't a man who'd appreciate some clingy female whining to be at his side. Heck, no guy did. But especially not a man like Dominic Laredo.

So she had to keep her feelings and her deepest desires to herself, keep him at a safe distance. And just savor every moment of this rapidly fleeting night. So for tonight, she'd enjoy Dominic—just like she'd enjoy wearing the gorgeous Cleopatra jewelry. She knew she'd be giving them all up soon.

The jewelry would be easy to walk away from. But what would she do when morning came and Dominic Laredo left her—forever?

After she put on the beautiful kimono Dominic had given her, she lay back down on the bed, propped up on her side, as he puttered around. Before she could ponder these sad thoughts much longer, Dominic once again aroused her curiosity. For he put away the Cleopatra costume and then turned to her with an enigmatic grin lighting up his face.

## Chapter Five

"Dominic," she asked, propped languidly against several pillows and enjoying the sight of his tidying up—in the nude. Great costume for cleaning up, she thought. If more people looked like him to clean the house, it might become the number one spectator sport in America. His body surely was the stuff of dreams. She'd have expected any man that buff to be the stereotypical dumb athlete. But Dominic was smart, funny, caring, not to mention enormously rich. Not to mention. Was this man missing anything? Not from where she was sitting. "You are Dominic again, aren't you?"

He grinned at her. "That depends. Do you want me to be Dominic again? Or Captain Hook? Or your slave? Or someone else?"

Though she was more than content to have him be Dominic, she wasn't about to admit it. Not when he seemed to be primed for more of his special fun and games. Of course, maybe she should up the interest by playing a little hard to get. She snorted to herself. Who was she kidding, after the way they'd been burning up the mattress—and the tub? He had to think she was the easiest piece of fluff in the universe. She blushed. Then she scolded herself for blushing, and vowed she'd be blush free for the rest of her time with him. No matter what the two of them did. She could go into permanent blush mode for the rest of her life after tonight.

The silence grew, but felt far from uncomfortable. "I see you're contemplating your response," he said, putting the Cleopatra wig away. Gwyn lightly fingered the necklace she was going to wear a bit longer. Dominic left the cabinet door open and came over to her, sitting near her on the bed and reaching out to massage her belly and legs. "Any thoughts in mind?"

"You expect me to think when you're doing that?" she asked with a quick chuckle.

He pulled his hand back. "You want me to stop?"

She snatched his hand and put it back where it had been. "I didn't say that."

He continued playing with her. "Any ideas at all of who you want me to be next?"

"You've raised my curiosity," she said, relaxing further into the pillows and giving herself up to enjoying the easy artistry of his large hands. "Do you have costumes for no matter what in that second cabinet?"

He smiled. "You've deflected my question for now, which is all right. All you ever have to do is say you don't want to answer. Gwyn, is there anything I can get you? More champagne? Something else to eat or drink?"

Thoughtful. He was thoughtful too. She couldn't imagine Pete ever thinking to offer her refreshments. Pete was more than content to let her be fully responsible for seeing to his needs. Come to think of it, that's the way he behaved in other areas too... "I'm not the only one deflecting questions here," she said. "But no, I couldn't eat or drink anything more. I really will answer your question later. First I want you to answer mine. What all do you have in that second cabinet?"

He shrugged. "Just a few baubles and clothes to make it possible to try out different roles while I'm on board. Sounds dull, doesn't it?"

"Dull?" She laughed dryly. That was one word that seemed to have no connection to Dominic. "No way. I'm amazed at what you were able to produce spontaneously when I said the name Cleopatra. And I wonder what else is in there?"

"Do you want to see now?" he asked, offering her his hand to climb out of the bed.

She shook her head, preferring to stay where she was over satisfying her curiosity. "Later, maybe. Right now I prefer to keep a bit of mystery."

"I'll have to remember that," he said, furrowing his brow. "The lady prefers a touch of mystery. But Gwyn, to answer your question. What I keep on this yacht is just a small sampling of all the toys and goodies I've collected. I keep some everywhere I live and at my private residences at all the resorts." He looked down for a moment, then looked her full in the eyes and added, "I hope I'll get a chance to show everything to you, soon."

Gwyn gazed up at him in wonder. Could he possibly be thinking of them being together beyond this one night? Or was his talk about a possible future just a ploy to get to her? Like he needed any ploy. In the immortal words of someone she'd seen in a forgettable movie, she was a done deal. He'd done her several times already, and she wasn't going to object to more of his lovemaking. Far from it.

On the other hand, she wasn't anybody's fool either. Maybe despite all his apparent good qualities, he also got off on raising people's hopes and then disappearing. Well she wasn't going to give him the chance to ruin her once-in-a-lifetime night with any asshole moves. She wouldn't let the word *future* take root anywhere in her heart. She was in this for the here and now, period.

It was time to change the subject again. She'd go back to his question. Who did she want him to be? Heck, she'd had her shot at being Cleopatra. She'd just tell him she wanted him to pick who to be next—and how to play out whatever scene he had in mind. She owed him that. A slight shiver trickled down her spine. She couldn't help thinking he might now go ahead and use the cuffs on her. How would that be? She'd loved using them on him, wasn't so sure how she'd feel being more bound than she'd been before. Or what if his secret fantasies were really kinky? Maybe she had a potential Mr. Hyde lurking below the surface of the apparent Dr. Jekyll? She shivered in anticipation of the unknown.

Well, one way or another, she was in for a night to remember. So though she could chicken out, her curiosity overruled any red flags of warning waving on the horizon.

"Your turn to pick," she said from her nest in the bed. "Tell me, Dominic," she purred in her most sultry voice. "Who do you want to be?"

His eyes glittered in what she could only describe as a wolfish leer. For a moment, she thought he was going to be a wolf and want her to be Little Red Riding Hood. Or would he want her to be Hood's grandmother? She smiled to herself remembering that the wolf had eaten the grandmother. Oh those sharp teeth and that tongue…

"Penny for your thoughts," he said, now widening the massage to include her whole torso, from under her breasts to just above her love triangle.

She shook her head. "It really is your turn, Dominic. More than anything, I want to hear who *you* want to be."

His hands slowed in their movements, lingering more now in each spot. "Having started the evening as Captain Hook, I feel tonight is the time for some of my darker heroes."

Gwyn raised an eyebrow. Perhaps they were going to delve into deeper, stranger waters than felt right to her—at least her conventional self. "Which dark hero?" she asked hoarsely.

"How about Al Capone?" he asked.

"Al Capone?" Somehow not at all what she'd imagined. "You feel like being a criminal bootlegger who machine guns people down?" she asked moving slightly away from him.

He shook his head. "That's not the aspect of Al that interests me when I'm with you," Dominic said. "Nor am I interested in exploring the glories of tax evasion tonight. Rather, did you know that Al Capone was a major ladies' man?"

Now he was rubbing her legs in a massage that simultaneously relaxed and aroused her. "No, I didn't know that," she said.

"Oh, yeah," he said, never losing the rhythm of his strokes. "And I believe he would have fallen for any flapper who looked like you. How could he have resisted? Did you ever think about the sex appeal the clothes of the twenties had? Those women looked so amazing with their short dresses and bobbed hair, I don't know how Al or anyone else had time for speakeasies and crime. What do you say? Will you be a flapper for my Al Capone?"

Like she was going to resist when he put it that way. Especially happy that nothing he had in mind involved machine guns, Gwyn let Dominic lead her out of the bed and over to the cabinet.

He opened the door. "Would you like to look in?"

For some reason she couldn't express even to herself, she hung back and said she was just as content to have him take out whatever they'd need. After wanting to look in the cabinet all night, she'd just chickened out.

"You sure?" he asked, grinning.

"Maybe later," she said.

"Whatever you want. I have a gorgeous dress for you," he said, taking out a padded hanger holding a lace-trimmed sky blue silk chemise that she guessed would fit her perfectly. Gwyn touched the fine silk of the dress and quickly realized this was a beautifully made, expensive garment just like the robe she'd worn as Cleopatra. Dominic also pulled out fine silk hose and beautiful shoes to match the dress. He handed her a pale blue silk garter belt, a long string of cultured pearls, a periwinkle blue cloche hat, sapphire earrings, and gold bangle bracelets. Everything was of the finest, most expensive cut and materials available. "Don't forget the makeup this time," he said, handing her a kit. "Glamorous flappers out to seduce Al Capone wouldn't be seen without full makeup. And how about being a redhead this time?" He handed her a wig of beautifully blended shades of red hair in a bob.

Gwyn felt like she was playing dress-up in Neiman Marcus or some other department store that was way beyond her budget—and probably would be for the rest of her life. She inhaled the fragrance of the cosmetics and clothes, willing herself to be fully in the moment. She'd have to pin her hair up to fit under the bob, which was much less full than the Cleopatra wig. She got started.

Dominic didn't stint on his own outfit either. As conceived by Dominic, Al Capone would have made the most exclusive of the best-dressed men's lists. He had an elegant white silk shirt, a three-piece black suit of the finest wool, a black derby, and even spats.

They both took lots of time to put on their costumes. Not needing to deal with cosmetics or fuss much with his hair, Dominic was ready before Gwyn. He watched her as she put on her makeup and gave a final pat to her wig.

By the time she rolled on her stockings and attached them to the garters, she'd truly begun to feel like a glamorous flapper—as if she'd just stepped off the set of the movie "Chicago".

"Gorgeous," Dominic said. "Gwyn, would you do me the honor of dancing with me?" he asked in a hoarse whisper.

She opened her eyes wide. "You want to do the Charleston?" she asked.

Dominic turned on his CD player. Gwyn could hear the sultry voice of a blues singer start up. "I had something a bit slower in mind," he murmured huskily.

That was definitely more her speed, too. She went into his arms and let him lead her. She closed her eyes, listening to the music, inhaling Dominic's scent, thrusting her hips against his erection, wedged so tightly on her belly as they swayed with tiny steps to the music enveloping them. The word "forever" slipped into her mind as they moved together to the music.

"You are incomparably beautiful," he whispered in her ear. "Do you feel what you do to me?" He pressed himself tighter to her, and her pussy went into spasms of ecstasy.

"Oh, Mr. Capone," she purred back to him. "I hear you say that to all the girls."

"Great, Gwyn," he said. "You're really getting into the role."

"Gwyn? Who's Gwyn, Mr. Capone? Have you forgotten my name already?"

Dominic laughed and held her tighter. "How could I forget your name? You're Amelia, right?

"See? You did know, Mr. Capone. That's right. That's me. Amelia...Smith."

"My dear Amelia, call me Al. Amelia and Al. That's us."

They danced to the rest of the song in silence, moving slower and slower as the song drew to its climax, their contentment with each other in sharp contrast to the singer's misery.

\* \* \* \* \*

Dominic couldn't believe how quickly and easily Gwyn fell in with his twenties fantasy. She looked so great in her flapper outfit—as if the designer had known she was making it for Gwyn. Dominic knew he'd never again be able to play this fantasy so perfectly with any other person. He hoped he wouldn't ever have to try to find another partner.

But how would Gwyn react to letting him bind her now? Before, he'd been confident she would join him on his pleasure path. Now, remembering the way she'd feared hurting him, he had a moment of doubt. And did she trust him enough for them to proceed? The way she'd held back from him raised doubt. She was too important to risk messing up with.

But for this beat of time, the music and the woman and the ambience were all he could have asked for. Like his partner, he gave himself up to the moment. But knowing himself as he did, he realized they'd just barely begun all he wanted for them to have together.

\* \* \* \* \*

After all their lovemaking of the night, Gwyn would not have believed she'd become so hot again for him so fast. Thoughts of her being a nymphomaniac and other unflattering titles flitted through her mind. Maybe she really was one of those insatiable creatures who were often the butt of male jokes. But she didn't let those thoughts linger for long. Why seek a negative name for what felt so right and so altogether fantastic? She was a woman with a man who seemed every bit as interested in mutual satisfaction as she was. No reason on earth to call herself names or try to fit any previously conceived labels to what they were doing. She'd do what she wanted tonight and find the language to talk about it some other time, when she was less pleasurably occupied. Which would probably be most of the rest of her life.

They continued to dance, drawing closer and closer for each successive song. Rubbing lightly against Dominic's erection as they moved around the room together in time to the perfect music nearly brought her to yet another orgasm. But now she wasn't feeling the first desperate hunger. She could savor the delicious feelings without shattering into a full screaming come. If anything, slowing her gathering climax would make it even more explosive.

She marveled at Dominic, who seemed to be able to stay hard for an incredibly long time. He neither grew soft nor pushed them ahead into another consummation. His restraint now turned her on almost as much as the music and his nearness. She wedged herself even closer, beginning to want to move their dance to a horizontal plane.

"Dominic," she murmured so softly in his ear that she almost exhaled his name like a butterfly sigh, "mmm. Was dancing like this Al Capone's *entire* fantasy?"

He moved slightly, thrusting his amazing cock against her so that she could nearly open her legs and straddle it as they danced. His lips brushed hers, starting a new fire. "This is just the beginning of what Al Capone wants to do with his beautiful doll in the flapper dress. Amelia, are you ready for what comes next?"

She shivered with desire and just a hint of apprehension. After all, Al Capone wasn't known for his angelic qualities. But she wasn't going to let some residual nervousness come between them. "Yes," she said. "I'm so ready."

He danced her over to the bed, sat her down, and rubbed his hands up and down her arms. "I've been waiting for you to say exactly that." His husky voice had her vibrating to the rhythm of his words. She ran her fingers over his full lips. He took her index finger in his mouth and sucked on it. Then he kissed her, his tongue exploring her mouth tentatively, as if he hadn't been there before. She savored his exploration, especially that he was taking time now to relearn the territory of her tongue, her teeth. And with a sigh, she joined him in this other dance, amazed at how new it felt to be kissing him. Before, she'd thought she could spend her life dancing with him. Now she knew she wanted to spend her life kissing him.

He gently took off her cloche and ran his fingers over her wig. It was fun being a redhead for this short time, playing with the whole new identity this simple change brought. When he touched her, no matter what color or style her hair was, she felt totally beautiful. She *was* totally beautiful.

"Let's get out of these clothes," he said softly. Gwyn nearly laughed. Putting on the clothes had been quite a chore only to be undone in a short time. Still, she was delighted to be getting naked with him again because of what would happen between them next. But everything she was wearing was so lovely, she didn't just want to throw it all off. She wanted to imbue each gesture with profound and special meaning for Dominic—and herself. And she wanted to feast her eyes on the way he took off his clothes.

"You first," she said.

He raised an eyebrow. "Oh, is it your turn to give orders again?" She might have worried that his question revealed some anger if the playful tone of his voice and his amused smile hadn't told her he was just having fun.

Playing along with the actual words he said, she hung her head and said, "I'm sorry, Al. I forgot my place. It's just that I so want to run my eyes and hands over your magnificent form, if I can get your *permission*." Then she grinned at him with such glee that he had to know any humility she was pretending was just part of their game.

"Hmm," he said, stroking his chin in mock meditation. With his cock bulging the way it did beneath the well-tailored slacks, Gwyn suspected he'd much prefer to be stroking that — or have her stroking it. Come to think of it, she'd prefer that too. She didn't know what turned her on more — touching him or watching him touch himself. But she wouldn't give him either satisfaction — yet.

"Tell you what," he said, somewhat breathlessly as his eyes fastened on what she was staring at. "I will undress first if you will permit me to watch you touch yourself under your dress while I remove my clothes."

She'd never touched herself in front of anyone else. She shivered with the anticipation of guilty pleasure, wondering if she should let Dominic into this tiny corner of her life. But her inner debate didn't last long. As she could already feel how moist her panties were with her desire for him, she wanted to say yes. But she also wanted to extend the deliciousness of this moment. To delay the moment of acquiescing, she played with the long string of pearls around her neck, twirling the shiny white orbs, enjoying the feel of them against her skin and in her fingers. And then, as he watched and waited, she put a small section of the pearls into her mouth and ran them across her tongue. She could see the bulge of his erection grow and she laughed. Another moment and his cock would explode the zipper.

"If you'd like," she said at last, giving the pearls a last lick, "I'll touch myself while I watch you take off your clothes, *Mr.* Capone," She winked at him.

"That's Al," he said hoarsely, running his hand over his straining cock and moaning. He undid his tie with nothing like the care Gwyn was taking of her garments.

Starting to really get into it, Gwyn gently kicked off her shoes and put one stockinged foot on the bed, exposing her silk-clad cunt to Dominic's avid gaze. With eager fingers she molded the cream colored silk of her panties into her tight wet folds, savoring the smooth coolness of the fine fabric as it lightly rubbed her gathering heat. She could practically feel and hear the sizzle—and, when she looked at Dominic, she was sure her pussy wasn't the only thing sizzling.

Now she pretended to ignore Al Capone as she became caught up in her little game, but she was hyper aware of him every moment. His eyes drank her in as he continued to strip off his own clothes in an uninspired manner. For a moment, she suspected he forgot his own role in their mutual play. "Al, I want to see you put on a show while I put on mine."

"Sorry," he said, for the moment putting a bit of drama into shrugging his vest off.

"Apology accepted," she breathed. Then he appeared to forget himself again as she lifted the string of pearls over her head and then languidly ran it over her cunt, pearl by pearl. She licked her lips, and whispered, "You're not naked yet."

He raised his eyebrow and cleared his throat. "Sorry again. A bargain is a bargain."

"And don't you forget it," she said. The touch of the pearls excited her, as did the feel of the silk. But what nearly brought her over the top was having this gorgeous man watching and showing her how much she turned him on.

By now Dominic had slipped off the suit jacket and vest, tossing them aside with a carelessness unusual for Dominic, but maybe typical of Al Capone. He slipped off his blue silk tie, and Gwyn fantasized how that tie would feel between her legs, massaging her hungry cunt. She'd now replaced the pearls with her own fingers. She slid her fingers up her thigh, gliding them up and down the sodden silk of her panties. Next she slipped two fingers in under the panties, gasping as flesh touched flesh. She brought her fingers, now slick with her moisture, up to her waiting lips and licked the juices off them. This was the way she tasted to him. Dominic groaned, telling her how much he wanted her—her taste, her scent, her feel. She held a finger out to him and beckoned him to her. As he moved, she closed her legs. "Still too many clothes there, Mr. Capone. Better put some hustle into it."

Watching her, he slid each shirt button through its meticulous hole, pulled the shirt tails out, and unfastened the heavy gold cuff links. Then he flung the shirt aside and stood magnificently bare-chested, his erection tenting out his pants with a promise she almost couldn't wait for him to fulfill. His shoes were long gone, which left only his pants. Gwyn wouldn't have minded taking those off him herself, but helping him undress wasn't part of their deal. He'd have to get out of his own pants before he could get into hers. Meanwhile, she wasn't doing half bad in the self-pleasure department. She feasted her eyes on him as she continued to finger her folds, amazed at how much fluid she was pumping out.

His hands were on his large heavy belt buckle, opening it. She maneuvered her hips around her fingers, thrusting her cunt up at him, her panties now tightly wedged along her pussy slit. The pressure of the panties on her clit nearly made her come, especially as she watched him finally lower his zipper—no easy feat with his erection distorting its teeth—and jump out of his pants.

Dominic's full, eager cock popped out of the fly of his black silk boxers. She wanted to grab him and take him into her, now. But with a strength of will she didn't know she had, she held back, wanting to see if it was possible to raise the level of excitement filling the room even further. In a blink, Dominic tossed off his shorts and stood before her, naked and gorgeous as some deity on Mount Olympus.

"Come here, Al Capone," she hissed, beckoning him with a finger wet with her fluids.

"Finish what you've started," he barked, his hand on his cock.

She looked at him coyly. "Myself? I don't think so. Not when I've got my big gorgeous Al Capone stud waiting in front of me with his big gorgeous cock."

He quickly gave up his brief resistance and came over to her. "Are you sure this is what you want now when you were doing such a good job yourself?"

She winked at him. "Oh, yeah. I'm so sure."

He growled, then removed her panties and ran his hand slowly across her burning slit, quickly followed by his tongue. She melted into him, her pussy nearly bursting with the pleasure of his touch. She rode him, her legs locked around his head, her fingers fisted in his hair. God, she wanted him to stay right where he was forever, licking her, making her throb with sensation. But he gently moved her legs apart and pulled away from her cunt, and she sighed—wanting him to stay, not secure enough to hold him where he was. But then he kissed her mouth hungrily, and she grew eager to see where he was going next. Dominic withdrew slightly from her, then took the pearls into his own mouth. Looking at her, he sucked the pearls, then pulled them out one by one and held them out to her.

"I want to put these in you," he said, displaying the pearls. "May I?" he asked, holding one up to the opening of her cunt.

She looked at him, dizzy with having to answer him. A frisson of hesitation snaked its way up her spine. "All of them?"

Her question seemed to surprise him. He answered with another. "Have you ever had pearls inside your treasure trove?"

"No," she said, drawing back slightly.

He stroked her pussy lips, bringing her to a higher level of anticipation. "You'll like it," he murmured. "Let me try just one pearl."

"Just one," she said, more unsure now than she'd felt about anything they'd done all night.

Watching him intently, Gwyn leaned back against the pillows and opened her legs, a bit cautiously at first. He stroked her gently with those magic hands. She lay back further and closed her eyes, rubbing herself against his fingers. He formed a fist and slid his knuckles along her folds, up to her throbbing nub. After he dipped his fingers into her moistness, he stroked her inner thighs bringing her juices outward. Gwyn melted, so relaxed that she nearly forgot about the pearls. Amazed that she could be so wet and that he could take her higher and higher with his touch, she opened her legs wider to him. And then she felt him slide one pearl into her, and she wondered why she'd been so hesitant. The hard smoothness of the beautiful gem lit a fire inside her, a whole new sensation she'd never known before. Wanting more, she slid toward Dominic with the pearl in her, and she licked her lips. "Another," she said. "Put another one in me," she ordered hoarsely.

He chuckled dryly. "Whatever you wish, my delicious oyster," he said, inserting a second pearl.

Twice as nice, she thought, but she still wanted to feel more and she told him so., With infinite slowness, he pushed in a third, then a fourth pearl. She closed her legs around the pearls and his hands. As he fingered her, he pulled slowly on the string of pearls, creating a heavenly friction inside her that left her gasping.

She was so on the edge, she fully expected to be screaming out an orgasm that would rock the yacht off its moorings and into orbit. She could swear Dominic knew just when she was going to let go, and he kept pulling her back from that edge, leading her higher and higher than she'd ever imagined possible.

"Al Capone, gangster man," she said, her voice drawing out his name. "I want…"

"What, my darling flapper, what do you want?" he asked, playing those pearls in her like a musical instrument.

She wanted the pleasure to last forever—and she wanted to come. She could feel her legs twitching in search of the satisfaction that had been building in her forever.

Dominic slowly pulled the pearls from her cunt and had her shivering in need and desire. Then he popped those pearls, now saturated with her moistness and her flavor, back in his mouth, his eyes closed as if he were feasting on the rarest of gourmet delights. Gwyn glowed in the realization that the pearls she'd had inside her were now filling his mouth with the taste of her excitement.

He never stopped holding her, touching her, bringing her along for the ride he'd been plotting. "I want to try something else," Dominic said, his voice low. "Something you've maybe never done before."

Gwyn knew that, even after all they'd done tonight, there was an awful lot she'd never done before. She'd been thrilled with everything else he'd introduced her to so far tonight. But the night was getting later, his voice lower, and her own sense of need and possibility sharper. Earlier he'd said he wouldn't do anything she didn't agree to…but maybe things were going to change now, as he realized how powerless she was to say no to him. Maybe he'd been hiding his true colors and now he was going to try to get her to do something that she wouldn't normally go along with. She summoned on what strength she still felt and pulled back a bit.

"Did you enjoy the pearls in your pussy?" His voice fell on her ears like warm honey.

She nodded slightly, definitely holding back from enthusiastic commitment on this one because she couldn't imagine where he was going.

"Let's try them now in your rear opening," he said softly, running his fingers and the pearls along her hip.

She stiffened, closing her lips in a moue of distaste. That particular request sobered her up faster than a full-body splash of ice water. "I don't think so," she said, repulsed at the thought of anyone putting anything in there.

He looked at her with his Captain Hook eyes, alternately gentle and challenging. "How about if I put just one in there, gently, just to see if you like it?" He held up the pearls now glistening with the mingled wetness from both of them.

Gwyn's heart was pounding with nervousness and also a tingle of possibility. He sounded so reasonable. Only one pearl. So small. They'd felt so good in her pussy. But her butt opening was also small, not to mention it smelled bad and was disgusting—even though she'd just had a thorough bath that included his washing her there. And the voice of excitement deep inside her kept reminding her that it would be okay, that he'd promised to stop at any time she wanted. Just one little pearl. The pearls had felt great inside her cunt.

He kept watching her, his eyes so big with his own desire.

"Okay," she said warily. "Just one. As long as you do everything slowly and promise you'll stop the moment I tell you to."

He inclined his head slightly in one of the positions he'd used as her slave. "Of course," he said, fingering her anus in a way she felt disturbingly delicious. Despite herself, she pressed back slightly against his questing finger.

"Are you ready?" he asked softly, his breath warm against her ear.

"Yes," she sighed. She rolled over on her side so that her tush was facing him.

He took the pearls in his mouth again and then ran them along the crack between her cheeks, which felt damn good. "I'm going to come in to you now," he said. She stiffened slightly, and he massaged her back there so she began to relax. Then he held a well-lubricated pearl at her anus, rolled it back and forth, and slowly began to probe inside the hole. She startled with the strange sensation, then, to her amazement, quickly grew to enjoy it. He let her stay with just the one pearl in her for several moments. She breathed slowly and deeply, getting used to it and to the idea of him touching her there. Then he asked, "Another, my love?"

She sighed. "Yes, all right. One more." He once again moved with great precision and slowness, sliding the string of small wet pearls up and down along the crack between her cheeks. The gentle tug on the pearl already in her had Gwyn twitching for more. By the time he inserted the second pearl, she was more than ready.

Dominic repeated the process with infinite patience. Hyper aware each step of the way, she agreed to having six of the perfect round white pearls up her anus. And then he tugged gently on the string of pearls within her, and she moaned her need for release.

"Now, my love," he said, covering her mouth with his in a deep searing kiss. Then he traveled down her body, trailing hot kisses. Every time she shifted to respond to his kiss, he gave a slight pull to the string of pearls, heightening her sensations so that she knew she'd die if she didn't come soon.

"Dominic," she moaned, as his warm lips and tongue began a new voyage into her deepest core. With his fingers he played with the pearls while he tongued her clit and the moist pink folds of her cunt. She tightened her legs around his head, riding his face, accelerating up to a pleasure peak that had her quaking. And when she began to come, she called out his name in a shriek. And Dominic slowly drew the string of pearls from her anus, one at a time, each one heightening her level of pleasure so that her screams did indeed rock his yacht...and him.

Gwyn came so hard, she amazed herself by bursting into tears. Tears? She *never* cried. What was this all about? She didn't want Dominic to think she was some weepy wimp who just turned on the water works. Far from being turned off, he became amazingly tender, kissing her tears away.

As she lay shuddering in his arms in the aftermath of her orgasm and the outburst of tears, he stroked her and petted her and murmured words of caring and praise and affection. While he crooned to her, she understood from him that he'd been thrilled to share in her earth-shaking come. How beautiful she was to him at this moment—every part of her.

Gwyn was still horrified at her tears. She began to apologize for crying. "Don't say you're sorry for letting go so thoroughly," he said, tracing the track of her tears with the tip of his finger.

"Is that what those tears are?" she asked.

"What else?" he asked, cupping her chin in his hand. "Do you think they're tears of sadness or being hurt?"

She laughed dryly, trying to gather the shards of her self around her. "The only sadness it could be is that I've never before had such an amazing experience," she said. "I feel sad for all the wasted years. But mostly I'm so happy and thrilled at what I just felt tonight." She needed to pull back from the intimacy of how much of herself she'd exposed to him, make it sound like all that had happened between them was just a really terrific form of sex.

He kissed her. "Such complex feelings."

"You're right," she said, kissing him back. She could get seriously hung up on this man, with whom she'd experienced so much in a few short hours. It was getting harder and harder to hold onto her emotions and keep anything of herself back from him. She'd probably be shedding rivers of tears about him afterwards, so she wasn't going to waste any more of tonight weeping. Even though it felt so amazing when he kissed away her tears. But she still had some of the night left, so she wasn't going to use up any more of it thinking of future regrets.

And first things first. The gorgeous man holding her in his arms had a massive erection. He'd had the same massive erection for ages. From what she knew about male anatomy, he could be in imminent danger of a major case of blue balls if they didn't do something soon. And she'd come so many times—way more than he had. It was time to even up that score.

She wet her finger with the tip of her tongue and softly stroked the head of his cock, which throbbed at the first slight pressure. He shuddered at her merest touch. His moan told her he was past ready for her attention.

"Your turn," she said. "And your fantasy."

"I was waiting for you to ask," he exhaled.

# Chapter Six

He smiled at her, skimming his finger down her side, raising shivers. Then he sat up. "I'm still Al Capone," he growled. "And you're my little chantoosie floozy."

She rubbed his leg with her still stockinged foot, feeling his erection press harder against her. "I can't sing a note," she admitted.

He laughed. "You don't have to," he said, nuzzling her.

"That's a relief." She propped herself up on her elbow. "So Mr. Capone, now that we know I can't sing, what is it you want me to do for my big bad bandit king?"

"Big bad bandit king?" he asked, his eyebrow raised. "I like that."

"I like this," she said, running her fingers lightly up and down his eager cock.

"And it's all for you, my pet," he said, easing away from her. He rose and crossed to his cabinets, took something out, and returned to the bed. He put down whatever he'd gotten before Gwyn had a chance to see it clearly. "Remember when I was your slave?"

"Very well," she said, "though I'd have thought you'd want me to forget, seeing as you're now a master criminal."

"Now that I have risen in the world, I want to give you pleasure the way you pleasured me before."

She leered at him, looking as if she remembered very distinctly how it felt to give and receive when she'd been the one free from restraints. And realizing that the moment when he'd want to turn those tables had probably arrived. "What do you have in mind?" she asked with a slight quaver in her voice.

"Simply this." He paused as if carefully choosing his next words. "I'd like to have you below me in very special bonds, so you can experience what I did. If that's acceptable to you. If it's not, please know you can tell me."

She inhaled sharply. Just moments before, he'd convinced her that having pearls up her anus would enhance her sensations. And he'd been more than right. But now he was urging her along to something new, something she'd formed previous opinions about. Earlier she'd admitted her long fascination with the implements they'd used together before. Though she now believed she preferred to be the one who wasn't restrained by those implements, it seemed only fair to give him a chance to cuff her. But some aspect of doing that scared the hell out of her.

Still, so far he'd lived up to his word in everything they'd done together—and he'd spent the night showing her she could trust him. There was no reason except for the warning flags her gut was sending up for her to start doubting him now.

"What do you mean to bind me with?" she asked, not completely able to suppress a slight trembling of her voice. She was sure he heard it too. She fully expected him to pull forth some highly polished metal implements.

"These are the first bindings," he said, sliding the silk hose off her legs. She shivered as he uncovered the flesh, both from the cool air and from the gentle pressure of his fingertips. Amazing that she'd remained even slightly dressed through all their lovemaking in this role play. Moving with quick deliberation, he divested her of her dress and her remaining undergarments. Now as naked as he was, she lay back against the pillows. He took one of the stockings and secured her right hand to the bedpost. "Is this all right?" he asked huskily.

She pulled her hand toward her, surprised at how the stocking became tighter around her wrist as she pulled, though the silk continued to caress her skin. "Yes," she said.

"May I also bind your left hand?" he asked, holding the stocking up.

She nodded her assent.

"Are those too tight?" he asked.

She wasn't sure. "How come the knots get stronger whenever I pull against them?"

He shrugged. "The nature of the knots. Do you want me to loosen them?"

"Not yet," she said, wanting to wait to see exactly how his fantasy would play out. "But maybe soon."

"Just say the word," he said. "Or maybe you'd like to have a signal to tell me to stop or to change something."

"Maybe a code word," she said, returning to the underlying playfulness of their interaction. "How about if I say the word Michigan?"

"Michigan?" he asked, pausing for a moment as he looked for something in a drawer. "Why Michigan?"

She shrugged. "I figured that's one word I can probably be sure I won't say tonight. Unless it's intentional."

"Michigan it is," he said, his eyes momentarily serious. He came over to her with two lengths of red silk streaming from his hands. "These are the binds for your feet. Do you want to touch them before I tie you down?"

She stroked the soft silk, nodded her approval before he wound them around her ankles, then attached them to the foot posts.

\* \* \* \* \*

Once he had her where he wanted her, Dominic feasted his eyes on Gwyn, extended in a delicious vulnerable spread-eagle pose on his bed, waiting for him. She was such a mix of innocent and adventurer. He loved knowing she had yet to taste so many experiences — and he'd be the one to introduce her to them. He thought of the way she'd responded to his use of the pearls. She'd had some hesitation, but she'd listened to his words, considered, then given her assent. And then she'd exploded with such ecstasy — and shared all her most intimate reactions with him.

Each moment with her, each different thing they did together, convinced him even more that Gwyn was the woman of his dreams. All those years when he'd been alone, constructing a fantasy world for others in his head and on his computer, she'd been the one he'd imagined at his side to share it with him.

Now he'd come to a decision: he would invite her to leave with him tomorrow. Dominic could just taste her enjoyment of all the new sights and sounds of the big wide world they'd wander together. Hell, just taking her around to his resorts would help him see them with new, fresh eyes.

Of course he knew she had a life already. There'd be stuff to deal with—her home, her work. He doubted that her involvement with Payne was anything serious. Dominic was absolutely sure it would take little time for her to wind up whatever obligations and commitments her simple life included. She had some job with a travel agency. Heck, he could buy her out of any contract, have his people make whatever arrangements were needed as far as her housing went.

The night was speeding away. Soon he'd have to talk to her about what lay beyond—about his plans for the future. But for now, well, his cock was signaling loud and clear that it was long overdue for release.

If Gwyn had any idea how magnificent she looked, her high, proud breasts jutting up at him, her feminine core open and glistening even now with desire and totally available to him, she'd play him big time. But she seemed oblivious as to her true beauty and desirableness. It was clear the way Payne treated her that he was an immature boy, little better than a high school punk, when it came to women. Gwyn deserved a man who could appreciate a woman like her. She watched his every move, her big green eyes pools of emerald desire. Caring. Admiration. And, did he dare think it, love. He could drown in her eyes and be a happy man as he went down for the third time.

He straddled her hips, his cock against her belly as he bent to kiss her face. Rock hard as he was, he didn't think he'd last too long. But even now, after all their loving, he wanted her to know he never thought just of his own pleasure, his own needs. He wanted to be sure she was thoroughly pleasured and satisfied before he reached his own climax.

So he kissed her first, savoring her lips and the taste of her. He probed her mouth with his tongue, gratified to feel her tongue probing right back at him. He stretched out full length on top of her, feeling her nipples bead and stiffen against him. Her heartbeat told him of her excitement, as did her rapid, shallow breathing and the delicious writhing that tested the limits of her bonds—and her lover.

He raised his ass up, his hands tight on her. He needed to be in her, now, the whole evening before this moment one long foreplay leading them here. With a groan, he rolled away from her, reached over to the night table for a condom, and with trembling fingers smoothed it over his waiting cock. As the head of his penis touched the rim of her cunt and she thrust herself up to him, he bit his lip to keep from starting his climax right then. Her warmth beckoned him, a solitary wayfarer who'd tarried far too long away from home. Because she was definitely his home.

With a moan, he thrust his cock into her, slowly, slowly, moving each millimeter with the most infinitesimal progress—his restraint the hardest thing he'd ever done. He imagined his cock a glacier, a river of ice slowly covering rich earth. But try as he might, he couldn't maintain that charade for very long because her heat was quickly melting whatever ice he could conjure.

With her legs bound, her pussy sheath was shorter than when she could wrap her legs around him. For a moment, he regretted the binding because he longed to feel her legs embrace him, suck him in deeper. But her writhing against the silk bindings and the sight of her trapped below him excited him too much for any regrets to last. As she tossed from side to side, her breathing grew ever shallower. Soon her hoarse panting had his bloodstream coursing at top speed. She moaned his name and reached her face up to him, wanting to taste his lips. He lowered his head and kissed her, sucking her lip, biting her, possessing her. She broke the kiss and lay back against the pillows for a moment, her eyes closed, a smile on her lips.

Dominic tried to maintain his slow rhythm as he moved in and out of her tight, hot narrowness, but his control was rapidly dissipating. He needed to thrust harder, faster, deeper to feed his enormous need for her. He nearly lost all control when he felt her cunt muscles ripple and clench him. Her groan and the way she tossed her head from side to side signaled that she was beginning to climax.

Not a moment too soon. He let go at last of the control he'd struggled for so long to maintain. Letting go, letting go. She screamed out his name and he paused for a moment to savor her orgasm. And then he resumed his movements, in and out, in and out, all pretense of control shattered. His whole body and soul tightened with his own climax. He spurted cum into the condom deep inside her — an ejaculation that left him drained, exhausted, mellow — for the moment. He collapsed on her, spent.

Though he wanted to linger, he couldn't stay where he was for long. They had things to talk about, and he couldn't think clearly on top of her. He carefully rolled off her, disappointed to have to move so soon.

"Michigan," she whispered as soon as he'd stretched out beside her.

"Michigan?" And then he remembered. Their code word. "What is it, Gwyn?"

"The bindings," she said. "Please take them off. Now. I want to hold you, and I can't."

Of course. She was still tied down. He quickly undid the knots, letting the pieces of silk slip away. "Do you want me to rub your ankles and wrists?" he asked.

She shook her head. "No, but I want to take off the wig now and let down my hair."

He helped her remove the bob and fluff up her hair. She carefully took off the earrings and pearls, which he put on the night table.

"Anything else?"

"Just hold me," she said.

He did exactly what she asked.

\* \* \* \* \*

Gwyn opened her arms to Dominic and savored the feel of his body cuddled against hers. She wasn't sure she liked being tied down as much as she'd liked having him tied down. Maybe they'd have to repeat both positions so she could decide. But she definitely loved having him next to her like this.

She laughed at getting into a major internal debate with herself about which position of being tied up she preferred. Maybe it helped her avoid thinking about what would be coming soon—the end of this magical night. The whole rest of her life, whatever she did and whomever she did it with would be a poor second.

She sighed, and he nestled closer. Her body felt so right molded against his powerful one. With him she felt all the things she'd never felt herself to be before: beautiful, desirable, a veritable sex kitten. Hell, with him, she was a much sexier and more dangerous cat. A panther or a leopard or something.

This was a night for her to be able to tell her daughters and granddaughters about. She chuckled. As if.

"Sleepy?" Dominic asked. "Mmm," she murmured, nuzzling her head in the perfect spot between his chest and his chin. She should be tired. She had no idea what time it was, but she was positive it had to be pretty close to morning. And then she'd have to go home and think about Dominic sailing off somewhere else, doing with another woman everything he'd done with her tonight. She felt vaguely like Cinderella, but that was a different story. And she wasn't going to leave a glass slipper behind.

Just her heart.

When she'd come to Dominic's quarters, she'd been pretty determined to go home and break off with Peter Payne. She thought of him again. He couldn't compare to Dominic, not on any level. But Pete was part of her real world, not some impossible fantasy like Dominic. In this case it was only Captain Hook, and not Peter Pan, who lived in Never Never Land. Exciting as this night had been, real life was about daily living—not about having some wild adventures with a man who had lots of expensive toys and read her like a book only he could open.

She'd just about convinced herself to leave the yacht with her upper lip stiff, her eyes dry, when Dominic said, "Come with me, Gwyn."

She laughed dryly. "I just did. Several times."

He kissed her and chuckled. "I don't mean sexually. Well, not just sexually."

"Huh?" Maybe her ears were playing tricks on her as she drifted toward sleep.

"Come with me, Gwyn, and see the world."

"What are you, a Navy recruiter?" she needed to show that she knew he was playing another game with her.

"Only for my own personal navy," he said, his voice totally serious.

"What game is this, Dominic?" she asked, wanting him to move to a safer topic.

"No game, Gwyn. Game time is over. I'm sailing off to the Caribbean early Monday. Want to check out my resorts in Puerto Rico and the Isla del Oro. I want you with me."

She drew away from him. "You're joking, and I have to tell you I don't like it."

"I never joke about checking out my resorts. Keeps the staff on their toes."

"Not about that," she said in a very small voice, annoyed that he was pretending to misunderstand her. "About me coming with you."

"I'm not joking," he said, stroking her face with his fingertips. "I mean every word I've said to you tonight."

Now her head really began to spin. "Michigan."

His hand froze where it was. "You want me to stop stroking your face?"

"Yes," she said. "It makes me crazy, and I can't think. But I also want you to stop fooling around."

"Fooling around? What do you mean?"

"About inviting me to come with you."

"I'm not fooling around, joking, playing games, or anything else like that. Gwyn, I've never been more serious in my life."

Her mind went racing with the possibilities he was throwing open to her—and that was far more dangerous than any of the role plays or toys he'd come up with. She glommed onto the practical, concrete aspects of her life that she could throw in his face as solid objections to his scheme. "You think I can just take off with you for some days of fun and sun like some playgirl? Dominic, I live in the real world. With a job and a cottage and plants that need watering..."

"Gwyn," he said softly, raising goose bumps up and down her spine, "I want you to come for way more than some days of fun and sun. I want us to get to know each other on every level. I want to be with you as you discover the big, beautiful world out there as well as the one inside you. We couldn't begin to do any of that in a few days."

Oh, he was really scaring her now—saying everything she wanted to hear. She really needed to keep her distance. "You mean a month? You expect the travel agency to hold my job if I take off for a month? And what about my cottage? I can't afford to pay rent on a place I'm not living in, especially if I'm not working." She was starting to get a headache with her effort to convince him—and herself—that she wasn't about to let him entrap her with his words.

Dominic shook his head. "Gwyn, please listen with your head and your heart. I want you with me now and for the future. Give up the job and the cottage and come with me."

She pulled away from him, sat up, and crossed her arms over her bare breasts. "Okay, fun's fun. But I'm not about to give up my home and my job just because you have a whim."

He sat up and put his arms around her, his face against hers. "I promise that if you ever need either a job or house again, I'll put all my resources into helping you."

She squirmed away from him, not enjoying what was evidently his weird sense of humor. "I don't like this new role play you're doing," she said, her voice very low to keep it from quivering.

He furrowed his brows. "I'm absolutely sincere about my invitation. I would never mess around like that—or lie to you."

She shook her head. "Why would you want *me* to go with *you*—for an unspecified chunk of the future?"

He hugged her again. "Oh, Gwyn, how can you ask that after everything we've had together tonight? Don't you know me at least a little bit?"

She wriggled away from him. "Come on. Let's face it. I'm nobody—and you're a rich big shot. Named to a magazine's list of the top fifty bachelors of all time. Heck, on everyone's A-list."

"Come on. You believe all that stuff?" he growled.

"Well, yeah. And don't tell me it's not true, at least some of it."

He sighed. "Any part of it that's true is way overrated."

"Easy for you to say. But from where I'm sitting, it all looks pretty damn good—and it doesn't look like it has any connection to my life." She moved away from him and got out of the bed.

He followed her. "Come back, Gwyn. Really, let's talk."

She sat back on the bed and perched at the edge with the top sheet drawn around her, now too aware of her nudity. She realized she had nothing to put on but the ridiculous Tinkerbell costume—or one of Dominic's get-ups. Heck, even the Tinkerbell costume didn't really belong to her. She pulled the silky top sheet tighter around her, but still felt totally exposed to him.

He sat next to her. "What can I do to convince you to hear me out?" he asked softly, for once keeping his hands to himself.

"I need some clothes," she said. "Real life clothes. Not a fantasy costume from one of your cabinets."

"Very well." He crossed to a built-in closet. She kept her eyes averted from his butt, which almost seemed to glow like a beacon in the darkened room. He opened the door and started rummaging. "I don't have much in the real clothes department that would fit you real well," he said. "Do you want to try some sweatpants and a T-shirt? They'll probably be far too big, but will work better than most anything else I can think of."

Those would work, she thought. Nobody could have a fantasy where she'd be wearing floppy sweatpants and a T-shirt. He handed her blue fleecy pants and a Fantasia Resorts in the Isla del Oro shirt. He was certainly right—the clothes were way too big. That was fine. She could roll up the pants legs and let the shirt hang. She felt a little self-conscious dressing in front of him, which was nuts. But she wasn't feeling particularly rational at this moment.

Once she had the clothes on, she sat back down on the bed. "Would you prefer it if I dress too?" he asked.

She could have feasted her eyes on him for days, but realized she could deal with him in a much more appropriate, adult way if he covered his bod. "Please."

He slipped into another pair of sweats, then sat next to her on the bed again—not touching, but close. "Gwyn," he said, "I don't want to take back what I said—which I mean as a very sincere invitation."

"Come on, Dominic. Let's say I did go off with you. Just left my job and house hanging in the wind. First of all, I care about the people I work with and rent from. But that's not your problem. Main thing is, what will happen when you get tired of me? Which I'm sure will happen real fast. Either you'll get bored, or you'll meet some A-list bachelorette, and I'll be instant history. You'll dump me off on some island in the Caribbean—or worse. I'll be broke, abandoned, and would have burned my bridges as far my job and house go. Can't say any of that is a particularly appealing prospect."

His eyes had grown very dark, nearly black. She thought he looked angry. "You don't have a very high opinion of me, do you?"

She shrugged. "I'm sure my opinion of you is pretty distorted right now, and I can't let that sway my thinking. I'm a realist. I know that's hard to believe after tonight, which feels like a fairy tale. But I have to ground my life in the real world, not let a random fantasy derail me. And you are not concerned about my life in the long run. All you want is someone for fun and games—'til you're ready for the next someone. No thank you." She got up and, being careful not to trip over her rolled up pants legs, began to pace.

He put his head in his hands. "Would it help if I told you that you mean far more to me than just a one-night stand or a short-time playmate?"

She waved her hands dismissively. "Well, you certainly have good manners. I'll give you that. But people like you have no idea what the lives of ordinary people like me are. Can't hold it against you. But trust me on this. You and I inhabit totally different universes. And never the twain will meet. Except for a night here and there, like this one was. But once I go home in the morning, this will all be just a memory. A beautiful memory, but..." Her voice trailed off.

He lounged back on the bed. "So you think my life has always been like this?" he asked, indicating all the luxuries around them. "That I grew up with money and privilege and women throwing themselves at me?"

"Well, yeah."

He shook his head. "Gwyn, I'm living the life I dreamed of when I was in high school and at university. 'Til just a few years ago, I was the typical nerd — great grades, too skinny and shy to have a social life. Dad was a clerk in a bank, Mum a homemaker. I have eight younger brothers and sisters, and we grew up in a small house in northern England. You do the arithmetic. My parents did their best, but luxury was not part of our lives." He got up and began to pace, careful to stay out of her way.

"Not only was I skinny and unathletic," he continued, "but I turned out to be good in math and science. Got great grades. Talk about a recipe for spending a lot of time alone. Which gave me loads of time to read. That's how I first learned about fantasies and different ways to fulfill them.

"With my academic skills, I got a great job just out of university. In those days, the computer business was hot. I was lucky. Got stock options, made great investments. I worked hard because I had nothing else to do. And soon I was on my way. During all those lonely years, I dreamed about making fantasies come true. Which is the idea behind all my businesses."

His story took her breath away. The way Dominic looked and acted, Gwyn had been positive he'd been groomed for success by a family with a long history of money and privilege. Hearing the truth complicated her thought processes. He wasn't just some fly-by-night playboy used to indulging himself in whatever he wanted. It had to have taken lots of guts and will to get to where he was. He was, after all, only a few years older than she was—and close to Pete's age.

"Dominic, thank you for telling me all this," she said, sitting down in his armchair. "I admire you tremendously for your accomplishments."

He continued pacing. "Thanks for admiring me. But does what I've told you change anything? Will you go with me?"

She shook her head sadly. Knowing about his background made him seem even more appealing than before, but that didn't alter the situation. "Now that you are so rich and successful, I'm afraid you've forgotten what it's like to be an ordinary person. You know, one who needs her job and spends most of her salary on a little house she thanks her stars to have found."

"Tell me about your work," he said, sitting down on the bed.

She suspected he was trying to divert her from her stand, but she was willing to go along for a bit. "I'm assistant manager at a local travel agency. It's kind of ironic that you're talking about my going away somewhere with you. I'm forever arranging trips for other people. Trips to exotic places—like the Mediterranean, North Africa. I even helped put together one junket to Antarctica."

"You like your work?"

"Oh, yeah."

"Why? Is it because you're so into helping people?"

"Well there is that," she said. "But mostly, I just enjoy the idea of getting to know about the places people go. Planning wonderful vacations, finding out about life in all the exotic corners of the world. It's almost as good as being able to go to them myself."

"*Almost* as good," he said. He looked as if he was going to say something more, then paused. "What about your house?"

"I have a nice little cottage I'm lucky to be able to rent."

"You don't own it."

She shook her head. "See? That's what I mean. You're clueless about reality. I'm grateful I can afford to rent a cute little place like that. It has much more character than some apartment, which is all most people in my age and economic group can manage."

"So what are the down sides to living in this cottage you don't own?"

"I'm fine as long as none of the owner's grandchildren decide they want to move in. She's only letting me stay there on the condition that I'll leave if they do."

"Oh. Doesn't sound like a bastion of security there."

"I can live with that sort of uncertainty," Gwyn said, sounding defensive.

"Sounds to me like a bit of a double standard going there."

She scowled at him. "I don't appreciate your judgments about my life."

"Sorry," he said. He came over to where she was sitting and reached out to touch her. She pulled back, and he began pacing again. "Gwyn, I can promise you I'd never dump you high and dry on some island or anywhere else. I have a feeling about our being together, but I know it's too soon for me to tell you all of it. All I can say is I want you to come with me. I promise I will always be fair and never hurt you. Can you trust me in this as you have all night with the other things we did?"

She inhaled sharply. Talk about making an offer she couldn't refuse. He wasn't making any extravagant promises about forever, and he did seem sensitive to her concerns about security—as much as a fabulously rich person could. He certainly knew how to say all the words that would melt her reservations, but only she could let go of those. The decision really was hers, and that gave her power here.

Wasn't she the one who was always saying there are no real guarantees in life?

What did she really have that kept her from saying yes to him? Her job—hardly unique. There were travel agencies everywhere. And, as she'd admitted to Dominic, she'd have to vacate her cute cottage at thirty days notice if any of the owner's grandkids decided to live there.

But then there was Pete. They hadn't spoken about him, but Pete still hung over her life like a shadow. Nothing Dominic said came close to sounding like the safe life she'd tried to convince herself she wanted—à la Aunt Nora. The life Pete Payne had been part of. But right now, Gwyn realized she didn't want to think about what Dominic *wasn't* offering—just what he *was*. Despite how hard her mind was working, weighing options, she yawned. She needed to get some sleep. Maybe when she had, choices would be a lot clearer. She told Dominic that.

"Sorry about that," he said. He offered her the bed. "May I sleep next to you, Gwyn?"

She believed that if she'd said no, he'd leave her to stay alone in the bed—even if he had to sleep on the floor. And that convinced her to have him next to her for this night. "Of course," she said.

"Kind of warm in here," he pointed out. "Do you want to stay dressed in those clothes?"

She looked down at her unglamorous outfit. "It is too warm for them. But Dominic, I really need to get some sleep now."

"I could use some too," he said, though he looked as wide awake as he had when she first met him.

Gwyn brushed her teeth, cleansed the last of the makeup off her face, and got undressed. Moments after she lay down, Dominic got naked and joined her.

He stretched out and got into position behind her, spooning Gwyn in the shelter of his arms. Sighing contentedly, she closed her eyes and fell into a deep sleep.

## Chapter Seven

Dawn came and went. Gwyn awoke to find herself wedged against Dominic's morning erection, his arms around her. Images of the night before danced in front of her eyes, flooding her senses with delicious tingles. Looked like Dominic was good to go again this morning. What a great way to start any day.

But she knew if they made love now, she'd never be able to think. And he'd challenged her. She had to make the most important decision of her life. Stay with him, sail off to an uncertain future? Could she really be that carefree? He'd said he would never abandon her in a bad situation. And last night had been all about trust. But now, in the light of morning, could she trust him on matters bigger than his treatment of a handcuffed lover?

Or should she continue with the life she'd been planning? The predictable one she'd carefully constructed to keep safe from the disaster her mother's life had turned out to be, the path Aunt Nora had raised her to avoid. Gwyn felt she was on really thin ice. Maybe her mother's genes were coming out after all — and she'd duplicate that woman's unfortunate fate.

Following Aunt Nora's design for her life, Gwyn had her job, her house, possibly a relationship with Pete — or with another man who was more her match than Dominic. Because Gwyn still couldn't help feeling Dominic was so way out of her league, they were the biggest social mismatch since Cinderella and the prince. And nobody really knew how happily-ever-after those two had ended up. Gwyn couldn't bring herself to totally believe in what Dominic proposed. Nothing he'd said had convinced her that the two of them would ever play in the same ball field—or fairy tale. Despite everything he'd shared about his life before he'd become a billionaire entrepreneur.

Dominic rolled over so they were facing. "Good morning, Gwyn," he said. He still looked gorgeous. Even bed hair didn't take away from his allure. "Did you sleep well?"

She yawned and stretched. "Very well, though not very long."

He grinned. "The night was taken up with other activities." He ran his hand along her bare arm. She closed her eyes, savoring the feel of his warm skin on hers, the coziness of sharing an early morning bed with him. "You said you were going to sleep on your decision." He was watching her carefully.

She looked at him. He was danger with a capital D, the king of the bad boys. He might tire of her in a week or a month. Nervous as that made her, now that he was touching her and looking at her, the cliché that you only go around once began to take hold of her, pushing out her image of Aunt Nora and fears of ending up like Mom. If Gwyn said no to Dominic, she might be safe, but she'd spend the rest of her life second-guessing herself. Curiosity got to her again. Also a healthy helping of lust. She'd push the fears aside and go for the gusto. She also wasn't going to play any games with him. "I have, Dominic."

"And? What, tell me."

"I will come with you." She said the words, and they felt right. For the first time since he'd made his offer, she could breathe easy.

He let out of whoop of joy that had the bed vibrating around them. Then he grabbed her in a big hug and kissed her. "Fantastic! Great! We sail tomorrow at the crack of dawn to the Caribbean. Have you ever been through the Panama Canal?"

She grabbed her face. "Yikes! Tomorrow? Geez, Dominic. Uh, maybe I need to spend a few weeks getting organized."

He gripped her arms. "Come with me. I don't want to you to miss a minute on the Bound for Pleasure. In a few weeks, I'll be back on terra firma, dealing with resort business full time. It might be months 'til I can sail again."

"I thought you spent most of the time on the yacht."

"Alas, another of the media myths about me." He grinned crookedly. "You'll find there are many."

"Do you have any idea how much I have to do to get ready to go with you?" She hopped out of bed.

He hopped out with her. "I have an idea. But Gwyn, you've made the big step and taken the decision. All the rest is doable in short easy bits. The job, the house. What can I do to help?" He went into executive mode, pursing his lips. "Let's see, as far as work goes. Tell your bosses I'll give them a special deal on Fantasia Resorts vacations—or even invite people from your agency to spend a few days at one of the resorts—all expenses paid. They can even fly on my private plane."

She rolled her eyes and chuckled. "That should ease their unhappiness at my just taking off with no notice. But there's still my house, my things…"

He was pacing. "Some of my crew can help you pack up, get things in storage—unless you want to take them with you."

"I'll accept that help, of course. And then there's Pete..."

He stopped. "Ah, yes, Payne. Your date last night." He whirled and looked at her. "How serious was your relationship with him?"

She shrugged, not sure how to answer. "We've gone out together for a while..."

"What are your feelings for the man?" He watched her intently.

She sighed. "In twenty words or less?"

"As many as you need." He folded his arms and a wary look crept into his eyes.

"I guess his needs and mine have been out of kilter for a while," Gwyn said slowly.

"Impressive epiphany." Dominic began pacing again. Even walking up and down the room in the nude, he looked powerful and in command. "Do you want me to speak to him?"

"I think that's my responsibility," she said, wondering how much Pete would care when she told him they were through. "Though I appreciate your offer to take it on. To be honest, I seriously doubt Pete will get too bent out of shape by my ending our relationship, such as it was."

"The man is obviously a fool, not that I'm complaining," Dominic said. "Well, his loss is my gain. I'll forever be grateful to him for bringing you to the party last night."

"And to think, I really didn't want to come." Had it only been last night that she'd first entered Dominic's world?

He beamed at her. "The power of synchronicity."

Dominic had a business meeting set up that morning — even on a Sunday — and Gwyn had tons to do to get ready to leave with him. So they both decided it would be best for her to get started. Ned, Dominic's assistant, would take her home and be on hand to help for whatever came up.

With so much to do, they both agreed they'd have to skip the lovemaking they'd much rather begin the day with. Gwyn quickly showered and dressed in another pair of sweat pants and a T-shirt — no underwear. It felt a little strange putting her black silk cape over her outfit, but not as weird as tottering around on her stiletto heels.

"Interesting ensemble," Dominic commented, taking her in his arms. He was still gloriously nude.

"You too," Gwyn said.

He laughed. Then he threw on a T-shirt and butt-hugging jeans to walk her out to the deck, where Ned was already waiting.

"Don't stay away too long," he called to Gwyn as she walked down the gangplank with Ned. "Phone me as soon as you know what you need."

She turned around and waved, excited now that she'd be returning to the yacht and her very own Captain Hook within hours.

* * * * *

Dominic watched 'til Gwyn and Ned disappeared from view. He frowned slightly. Though he believed in the power of his positive thoughts, he couldn't ignore the vague suspicion that everything had gone too smoothly up to now. He'd met Gwyn, and so far they'd turned out to be more than compatible on the most intimate level. She evidently wasn't emotionally involved with Peter Payne. Dominic's dreams about finding the right woman were finally coming true.

So why his creeping uneasiness? Rational computer scientist and businessman that he was, Dominic still had complete faith in his own intuitiveness. And something was definitely bothering him.

Of course he'd have preferred to go to her home with her himself. Dominic smiled to himself. That was part of his needing to be in absolute control. Bloody hell, even his mother had recognized this in his nature. He trusted Ned Smithers totally, no question about that. Ned would drive Gwyn to her home in Dominic's red Jaguar. Once Ned knew how many of her things Gwyn wanted to bring with her, he'd phone and tell Dominic to send a van or a larger truck. They could get a storage place for whatever Gwyn didn't choose to bring aboard. And Dominic was sure Gwyn's employers would be amenable to his offers. All that would go like clockwork.

But Peter Payne troubled him. Dominic could never believe any man would give a woman like Gwyn up without a fight. Payne was a bit of a wild card. Dominic wouldn't be able to relax fully 'til he knew Gwyn had severed her ties with Payne—consigned her personal Peter Pan to his particular Never Never Land.

Dominic went back to his cabin to shower and dress for his appointment with Laura, the rep he'd met Friday. He'd promised to complete their negotiations before he left San Diego, which he was planning to do before this time the next day—with Gwyn at his side.

\* \* \* \* \*

Gwyn had never ridden in a Jaguar before. Though she usually didn't pay much attention to cars, the sleek lines of Dominic's thrilled her newly heightened senses. She ran her fingers over the glossy finish before she got in. Ned was holding the door for her. She'd also never before been driven by a chauffeur. Ned wasn't wearing one of those hats, but for all intents and purposes, he was her chauffeur today.

Gwyn leaned back in the caramel leather seat and closed her eyes, soaking up the atmosphere. The car smelled new. Soft jazz issued forth from the CD player. Gwyn couldn't believe the contrast between how she'd left home for the party less than twenty-four hours before and how she was now returning there. She felt like she was living some fairy tale movie script. Part of her hoped she wouldn't wake up any time soon.

"Is this your street, miss?" Ned asked. Like Dominic, he spoke with a British accent.

"Yes. My house is in the middle of the block," she said.

Funny, she didn't know nearly as much about Dominic as she'd have expected to know of a man she was about to leave home with. Though he'd told her he was from the North of England, she didn't have any more specific information—like what town or city he'd grown up in or what life up there was like. He'd told her he was the oldest from a large family, but had the Laredos been happy together or dysfunctional? Gwyn's rational self warned that her ignorance might come back soon and bite her on the tush.

Her reverie came to an abrupt end when they pulled up to her cottage. Sprawled there on the small patch of lawn like the leftovers from a wild party was a pile of what looked like sleeping bodies. Gwyn groaned. Pete's Jeep was parked at the curb. Peter Pan, Spiderman, and the Hulk were stretched out on the grass. Gwyn felt like she'd been transported from Cinderella at the ball to Saturday morning cartoons.

Ned helped her out of the car and nodded to the group. "Do you know who those men are, miss?"

Gwyn straightened up. "Unfortunately, I do."

"Do you want me to call the authorities to have them removed?"

Gwyn shook her head. "No, thank you. I'll take care of it. Why don't you just wait here in the car."

"Very well," he said, getting back behind the wheel. He didn't look too happy with her instructions.

Gwyn, her heels sinking into the grass, walked over to the rhythmically snoring trio. She squatted next to Pete and began to shake him. "Wake up," she repeated until he finally began to stir. The other two continued snoring in disharmony.

Pete began to yawn, scratch, and look around, disoriented. Then his eyes opened wide as he figured out where he was, and he sprang up. His cap was totally askew, but otherwise his outfit looked remarkably the way it had last night. Gwyn rose with him. He put his hands on her shoulders and looked her up and down, frowning. "Where have you been?" he asked, nearly bowling her over with morning-after party breath. "Are you just getting home from Laredo's yacht now?" He looked accusingly at her.

Gwyn, feeling assaulted, stepped back. "Good morning to you too, Pete Payne," she said.

"When did you get home?" he asked, scowling.

"How long have you been here?" she asked right back.

Pete rasped his hand across his morning scratchy beard. "Me and the guys came here straight from the party," he spat out. "I wanted to be here when you arrived."

"Why?"

"What do you mean, why?" He looked wounded. "Wanted to make sure you were safe. Realized I shouldn't have left you with Dominic Laredo. Guy's too dangerous around women."

Gwyn wanted to laugh. Pete didn't know the half of it.

"I appreciate your concern," she said, "but it really wasn't necessary. As you can see, I'm fine."

He looked her up and down again. "Why are you wearing sweats and not your Tinkerbell outfit?"

"I'm more comfortable in this."

"We could have won that contest, but you pooped out," he accused. "The people who did win didn't look half as good as us."

She didn't want to get in this discussion with him now. She just wanted to get moving with all she had to accomplish. "This is no good, Pete. Why don't you tell your friends to go home? Come in. We need to talk."

He shrugged. "Ah, let them sleep it off. They'll get up on their own soon anyway. Your lawn's not ideal for sleeping."

"Come inside then. I'll make us breakfast." She glanced over to the curb and saw Ned still sitting in the driver's seat, watching her and Pete. "Go ahead. I'll be right there."

Tired of battling her lawn, she took off her shoes and went over to the Jag to tell Ned what was going on. "I'm going in the house now with one of the men, Pete. I need to talk to him. Won't take long."

"Is that advisable, miss?" Ned's brows furrowed with concern.

She smiled. "It's all right. I know him. Ned, I'll be making some coffee and breakfast. Anything I can get you?"

The older man smiled. "Thanks, miss. That's very kind of you. Actually had a bit of breakfast before, but I'd be happy for some coffee. Black."

"I'll be out with it as soon as it's made."

Pete was lounging at the table, his long tights-clad legs stretched out. Gwyn rejected her first plan, to make fancy French toast. She didn't want to spend the time needed to put together a really nice breakfast. Cold cereal and milk, along with coffee, of course, would do just fine. She got the coffee brewing, then put out two bowls, spoons, milk in its carton, Frosted Flakes for Pete and granola for herself. Pete poured himself cereal and began eating in sullen silence. As soon as the coffee was brewed, Gwyn poured a mug for Ned and went to the door. "I'll be right back," she said when Pete looked up inquiringly. "You can pour yourself a cup."

"Where are you going?"

"I want to take Ned, Mr. Laredo's driver, some coffee."

Pete drew his brows together. "Why did Laredo's driver bring you home this morning? And why is he waiting around?"

"We'll talk as soon as I get back," she said, hurrying out to Ned so he'd get the coffee while it was still hot.

"Thank you, miss," he said, carefully taking the mug from her. He took a big sip and sighed. "Is there anything I can do to help you right now?"

"I'm fine, Ned. I'm going to eat a quick breakfast. I should know more about the schedule after that. So why don't you relax a bit. Would you like me to bring you a paper or a magazine?"

"Very kind of you, miss, but I'm fine. Do let me know as soon as possible if you want Mr. Laredo to send a van or a truck for your things. I know he's anxious to get everything organized."

Gwyn assured Ned that she'd keep him posted. Walking back to the house, she noticed the two Super Heroes still fast asleep.

Now that she was actually with Pete, she dreaded telling him that their relationship was over. Even in situations like theirs, where no real commitment ever existed, breaking up was no picnic. She squared her shoulders and went back inside.

Pete was pouring himself a second bowl of cereal. Gwyn wasn't really hungry. She poured herself some coffee, then sat down opposite Pete. He looked at her. Gwyn smiled to herself as she sipped her coffee. He really did resemble Peter Pan. Funny how she'd never noticed before.

"Okay. So let's talk, Gwyn. For starters, where have you been all night?"

Might as well cut to the chase, she thought. "I was on the Bound for Pleasure. With Dominic Laredo."

He put down his spoon and frowned at her. "You were there *all* night with him?"

She nodded.

Pete appeared to digest this news for several heartbeats. "Uh, did he try anything... *funny?*"

She nearly choked on her coffee. She supposed it would be inaccurate to call anything that had passed between them *funny*.

Pete was drumming his fingers on the table, frowning at her. "The guy's got a terrible reputation. Dressing like Captain Hook showed his true colors."

Gwyn thought back to Dominic doffing his tricorne, to him showing her his hook and his handcuffs, and the uses they'd put those cuffs to. "Stop," she said to Pete. "Just stop."

He looked at her in surprise. "You want me to stop talking?"

Gwyn nodded. "Pete, just listen. I have to be honest with you." She paused to choose her words. "Last night I was *with* Dominic Laredo—in every sense of the word. This morning I woke up in his arms. And I'm going away with him tomorrow."

Pete jumped up and threw down his spoon, splashing milk and bits of cereal all over the table. "The hell you are. I can't believe it. You were with that bastard all last night? He pretended to take you somewhere to rest, and all the time he was..." Pete bounded over to her side of the table and looked like he was going to grab her and throttle her.

"Stop, Pete! " she said, scrambling out of her chair and out of his reach. When Pete had frozen where he was, she pointed to the chair he'd nearly turned over. "Sit back down so we can finish talking like adults."

Pete started to say something, glared, then shrugged, and sat down.

Gwyn took a deep breath and returned to her own chair. "I'm not going to go into details about last night. But I've thought a lot about my life, maybe more in the last twenty-four hours than in years. And I've realized a whole lot about myself, things I hadn't wanted to face before. And Pete, it's clear to me that you and I are over. Finished. It just hasn't been working out, and it's never going to. So please understand, and maybe you can even be happy for me." She held out her hands to him to ask for his good wishes. "I've decided to take Dominic up on his invitation — and see the world with him."

"Dominic," Pete echoed, his voice sounding ugly and his eyes narrowing to two blue pinpoints.

Clearly Pete wasn't interested in ending their relationship on a high note. But the look on his face was far nastier than Gwyn would have expected, given the way he'd always taken her for granted. Where was Pete coming from now? "Look, I realize this is a surprise for you. I'm trying to make things as easy for everyone as I can. And I've got to get busy so we can take off tomorrow. I just came back home to arrange what I need to."

Pete rolled his eyes. "Oh, and I suppose telling me your grand plans is just one of those arrangements you need to see to?"

Gwyn winced. "I'd give anything not to have to hurt your feelings. But you must realize, even without Dominic, it's over between us."

"That's news to me. I thought we had something good going."

Gwyn couldn't believe it. Had the two of them ever really been on the same page? "Pete, face it. You and I together have been headed exactly nowhere for a long time. That was clear to me last night, even before Dominic came over to me."

He shook his head, reached across the table, and put his hand around her wrist. She thought she saw genuine pain in his eyes. "I don't know anything like that," he said in a near growl. "I thought things were great between us. Up 'til I took you on that thieving pirate's tub."

Gwyn shrugged off his hand. She still couldn't believe how oblivious he was to her needs. "Things haven't been great. Not even okay. Take Friday night, when I slaved to make you a nice dinner, then you just left me to go be with your buddies."

"You're going to hold one night against me? What about all the times I stayed?"

"It's not just the one night. It's how deaf and blind you've been to my needs for ages." How was she going to prove to him in a few minutes what he hadn't been able to get in two years? "Look, Pete. Maybe the bottom line is I'm just not the right woman to get you to respond. You've never understood what I wanted when I told you. And there's been lots I've never felt comfortable telling you."

"Like what?" he challenged, folding his arms in front of him and leaning back in his chair with his legs splayed out in front of him. "What haven't you been comfortable telling me?"

She squirmed. "Fantasies. Needs that Dominic sensed as soon as he met me."

Pete's mouth twisted into an ugly sneer. "That guy's screwed every broad from here to London and back. Not to mention running Fantasia Resorts. He didn't *sense* anything. He *knows* women's minds. That's what's made him a millionaire. A billionaire. And all you are is one more notch in his money clip."

Pete's accusations hit too close to her own fears to be waved off. Gwyn pushed away the doubts about her experience that were already beginning to infiltrate her joy at the prospect of being with Dominic. "That's not fair, Pete, or true. You don't know anything about what happened between us."

He laughed harshly. "You're talking about being fair? After you went to the party as my date and abandoned me for Mr. Got-Bucks?"

"Abandoned?" she said, cringing as she heard her voice rise. "You want to talk about abandoned? You left me stuck at a party where I knew no one so you could laugh it up with your buddies." She looked down at her hands. "You know I have abandonment issues, what with the way my mother left me..."

"All you had to do was come over and join us," he thundered. "I was trying to be considerate because I know how much football bores you."

"I *did* come over. You told me to go look for the guys' dates—who I never did manage to find."

"That's not my fault."

"No. But you shouldn't have put me in that position in the first place. Why couldn't you just have waited for another time to talk to them about the friggin' football?" she hissed. "It's not as if you don't see them every day at work. And you're all constantly e-mailing each other."

Pete started to say something, then bit his lip. "Sorry, Gwyn," he said. "I wasn't thinking."

She nearly fainted. In all their time together, Pete had never apologized for anything. He looked contrite. Was it possible he'd changed? "Apology accepted, Pete." She reached out her hand to him. "I'm happy we'll be able to part on a good note, as friends."

He kissed her hand, something else he'd never done before. Gwyn shivered as goose bumps raced up and down her spine. She realized with some irony that she'd started training Pete well. The next woman in his life would probably benefit from her hard work. "What do you mean, *part?*" he asked, his eyes overflowing with innocence and adoration.

She pulled her hand back. "I guess it didn't register. Dominic invited me to sail away with him, and I've accepted. We leave tomorrow morning. I have to make the necessary arrangements about my house and job today."

He shook his head. "I guess you're the one who things aren't registering for," he said. "But listen up, Gwyn. Dominic Laredo is every woman's worst nightmare. You'd be safer jogging blindfolded on the freeway than going off with him. Even if you and I are really through, which I don't accept. Don't go off with him."

"I'm tired of trying to play it safe. Unless you hide cowering under your bed, life is filled with taking chances," she said.

"Which is why I've decided to take one with you," he responded. "Gwyn Verde, marry me."

She nearly fell off her chair. She'd wanted some romance, some indication that Pete cared for her beyond the regular sex. But marriage had been further outside her thought processes than a vacation at Fantasia Resorts. Gwyn was speechless.

"You want me to get down on my knees, Gwyn? I will." He went over to her and knelt down, taking her hands in his. She remembered when she'd knelt in front of him, just two nights before, and taken his cock in her mouth. And how he'd left her afterward.

"Marry me, Gwyn. I'll get you a house with a white picket fence. I'll even give you an engagement ring, as soon as I buy one. What do you say? My legs are beginning to cramp."

She laughed. "Stand up, Pete."

He did.

Now her head was really whirling. Two such different proposals in the space of less then twenty-four hours. Gwyn felt like she'd landed in some alternative universe.

Pete wanted to marry her. Dominic had dazzled her and convinced her to walk away from her life in San Diego and take off with him. She'd felt so alive with Dominic — from the lovemaking and the talk and the sheer wonder of being with him. But how much of that was just an illusion Dominic continuously spun out to keep his enormous ego fed?

This morning was like the sting of a cold shower. Now that she'd explored some of her wildest fantasies, maybe it was finally time for Gwyn to grow up. She knew all the details of how life would be with Pete. She knew where she'd be living, the texture of everyday life. She knew Pete's good points and his rough spots. He'd proposed — marriage, a real and tangible bond. Maybe she needed to listen to him and to say yes. Maybe it was time to consign her night with Dominic to her memories — which had been her intention for most of their...interlude.

Or, maybe she needed to choose none of the above.

"You haven't answered," Pete said.

"You have to give a girl a chance to think," she said, pushing herself back from him a bit. "After all, it's not every day someone asks her the most important question of her life."

He gave her his crooked, boyish grin, the one that always had melted her heart in the past. Now that she was back on terra firma, in her own cottage, surrounded by the reality of her life, the danger of what she'd been about to do came crashing down around her. Pete was offering her a sure thing. Surely Aunt Nora would have approved. Gwyn's mature, rational self stepped up to the helm of her sinking lifeboat.

But she couldn't bring her mouth to form the word yes. Every time she opened her lips to produce the one syllable he was waiting to hear, she felt too strong a pang of loss. She couldn't wrap her mind around believing she'd never again be with her pirate captain, her love slave, her gangster boss — her Dominic. The silence stretched embarrassingly. Finally, Gwyn said, "Pete, I need time. I promise, I won't do anything rash or without telling you."

He looked less than thrilled with her hesitation. "You're not going to just take off?"

Gwyn sighed. "No. So first I need to go out to tell the driver to leave. No sense having him hang around."

"Right," Pete said. "I'll go with you. Then we can tell the Super Heroes to go home. Their guard duties are done."

Gwyn chuckled. Those Super Heroes had done an impressive job of guarding.

When Gwyn and Pete arrived at the Jag, Ned Smithers had just ended a phone call. He got out of the car, handed Gwyn the empty coffee mug, and thanked her. "What can I do for you now, miss?" he asked, looking from Gwyn to Pete and back.

"Actually," she said, blushing, "you can go back to the yacht. There's nothing further for you to do here."

"Nothing further, miss?" Ned's face remained impassive, but his voice sounded a bit higher than before. "But don't you need me to order a vehicle to transport your things? I've already arranged for a storage facility, though I can change that if the size doesn't suit you."

"Thank you so much for everything," Gwyn said, feeling unwelcome tears start to rise. "Please, go back to the yacht. Tell Mr. Laredo thanks, but no thanks. He'll understand."

Ned shook his head. "Very well, miss. If you're sure." He turned on the ignition, then turned it off. "If you change your mind or think of anything at all, please contact me on the car phone." He gave her a small white card with his name and the number. Then he drove off.

"Laredo's lackey," Pete muttered under his breath.

"He's really a very sweet man," Gwyn murmured.

"Whatever," Pete said. He went over to his buddies. Spiderman was already showing signs of life. Gwyn supposed it was nice that Pete had such good friends. After all, they'd been willing to spend an uncomfortable night sleeping on a lawn for him. But she couldn't help wishing he made as much time and effort to be with her as with them.

When they came back to the house, Pete sat down on the couch, Gwyn in one of the armchairs. She should have felt relieved, but all she felt was empty. "You haven't given me your answer yet," Pete reminded her.

"It's only been ten minutes," Gwyn said. "I need to think, and you have to give me the time and space."

"I thought a marriage proposal was what you wanted," Pete snapped.

Gwyn shook her head slowly. Life had just become so much more complicated. "I'm flattered, Pete. But what I wanted from you, what I needed from you, was romance. Caring. I wanted to feel that you think about me, try to plan ways to let me know you care."

"A proposal of marriage doesn't do that for you?"

"I think that's premature," she said. "After last night, I feel like you and I don't really know each other. And maybe we need to get to know each other a lot better before we think about marriage or any commitment."

"But you felt you got to know Laredo so well in one night that you were willing to chuck everything to be with him."

"I really don't want to talk about…"

Pete jumped up and began pacing. "What the hell happened between you two? Must have been some dynamite, mind-blowing sex to have you all turned inside out today. What's the guy have, a ten-inch cock? If so, he probably bought four inches. Had himself surgically enhanced or something."

"Sit down, Pete. You're making me dizzy with your pacing."

Pete perched at the edge of the couch, looking like he was going to jump out of his skin. "You've got to tell me, Gwyn. What exactly happened between you two? You owe it to me."

She shook her head. "If you keep talking like this, I'm going to ask you to leave, Pete."

"Oh, no. Listen, if it's the sex, you've got to give me a chance to show you. Anything he can do, I can do better, harder, faster, longer." He got up and came over to her, holding out his hand. "Come on, Gwyn. Let's take this to the bedroom. Let me show you what and who I am. I'll make you forget you ever met Dominic Laredo." His voice had grown very low.

This was too much. Gwyn jumped up and waved Pete away from her. "Pete, I want you to leave now." When he'd backed off a bit, she continued. "Look, I don't know what's going to happen between the two of us. But if you stay much longer, I'm sure we'll both regret what happens. And then there really won't be any future for us."

Just then someone started hammering on the door, demanding to be let in.

"Don't answer that," Pete ordered.

Gwyn crossed to the door and opened it. Looking like Captain Hook right before he hurled captives into the sea, Dominic stormed in.

## Chapter Eight

Dominic glared at Gwyn, raised his arms as if to shake her, then put them down again. "What the hell happened? Why did you send Ned back to the yacht alone?"

Gwyn took a deep breath. This was going to be the really hard part, telling Dominic she wasn't leaving with him after all. Especially with Pete glowering across the room. Seeing Dominic in her living room, a tidal wave of feeling for him crashed and broke over Gwyn. She knew it would take a long time to get over him. Maybe she never would. "I'm sorry," she said, softly. "I changed my mind and…"

"Changed your mind?" he thundered, pacing. "We discussed everything, arranged everything…"

"You heard the lady," Pete shouted, leaping into Dominic's face. "She changed her mind. She's going to marry me. Now get the hell out of here."

Gwyn shook her head. "I have *not* accepted your proposal."

"Yet." Pete hissed. "You haven't accepted my proposal yet. You haven't rejected it either." He looked almost as murderous as Dominic. "You will," he said. "You just said you needed time and space. Unlike Laredo, I'm giving you time and space. Get the fuck out, Laredo."

"I'm not going anywhere 'til I've had a chance to talk to Gwyn," Dominic snarled.

"She doesn't want to talk to you," Pete snarled back.

Dominic turned to Gwyn. "The lady can speak for herself," he said, lowering his voice.

"This is going to speak for her," Pete said. He drew his fist back and punched Dominic in the gut.

Gwyn screamed. Dominic doubled over with a quick grunt then stood up and held his hands in defensive position in front of his face. "Don't act like a child, Payne," he panted. "We can talk this out like adults."

Pete threw another fist out, which Dominic blocked. Then Dominic punched him in the stomach and Pete caved. His fists still clenched, Dominic towered over him. Pete started to get up, looking determined to resume the battle.

"Stop!" Gwyn jumped between them and held her hands out to keep them apart. She couldn't believe the two of them were fighting over her. Though she had to admit part of her was thrilled—after all, how many women ever have two good-looking men get into a fistfight over them?—her adult rational self was horrified. These two clowns could get hurt if they didn't stop. And the last thing she wanted was for either of them to suffer any more damage than she'd already inflicted on them. "Dominic, you go sit in that corner." She pointed to make sure he knew where to direct himself. "Pete, you go sit in the other."

The two men glared at each other, but each headed to the spot she'd designated. Gwyn took referee position between them. "Does anybody need ice?"

Dominic nodded. "I could use some," he said. "Payne, you pack a mean punch."

Pete slitted his eyes, as if expecting Dominic to insult him. When Dominic didn't say anything else, he nodded to Gwyn. "Me too."

"You'd better both sit where you are while I go to the kitchen," she ordered. "I'll throw out anyone who moves so much as a muscle." She gave them both her best school principal glare, then, muttering to herself, went to the kitchen. She returned quickly with a bag of frozen green beans wrapped in a dishtowel for Dominic; Pete got the frozen peas. She watched as each man molded the bag to his midsection and sat back. Then she dragged out the small footstool and sat half way between them.

Dominic looked from Gwyn to Pete. "Gwyn, tell me what's going on," he said softly, his eyes burning.

Before she could answer, Pete chimed in. "We're going to get engaged, Laredo. You know, engaged to get married. You didn't have the class to leave my date alone last night, but maybe you'll at least respect our being engaged. So leave my almost fiancée alone. In fact, why don't you just leave, period. Your presence is not wanted here. Oh, by the way. You want my resignation, it's yours. As of Monday morning." Pete jutted out his jaw and might have looked tough if he weren't pressing the frozen peas against his bare gut. More than ever, he now looked like the Jolly Green Giant.

Dominic held up a hand in a "Stop" position and shook his head. "Payne, I expect to keep whatever happens between us here as strictly personal. No professional repercussions." He turned to Gwyn. "A few hours ago, you were set to sail off into the sunset, or in our case the sunrise, with me. Now you turn out to be Payne's fiancée. What's happened?"

Pete started to rise, but sank back in his chair when Gwyn glared at him. His face took on an arrogant sneer. "She's choosing the better man. Deal with it, Laredo. Don't let the door hit your ass on your way out."

"I haven't said yes, Pete," Gwyn pointed out again. She couldn't believe the way Pete was talking to Dominic. His rudeness was even more unbelievable because Dominic was his boss. She could see Dominic was struggling to act like a gentleman. Her heart did a flip. It wasn't just Dominic's looks that got her knees wobbly and her hormones hopping. But she couldn't let herself get carried away by his suaveness or suavity or whatever the hell it was. Seeing that Pete was starting to get out of his chair in a threatening manner, she added, "Pete, behave." He sat back and moved the frozen peas around.

"Dominic, I'm really sorry," she said, only too aware of how inadequate her words were. "I guess it doesn't make a difference if I say a lot or just a little. Pete did propose to me this morning. I haven't accepted him. But now I realize I need more time before I make any huge decision."

She could see the muscles working in Dominic's clenched jaw. "You're asking more from me than you can know," he said softly. "I thought we understood each other. Now you're telling me I was wrong. I hate being wrong."

"I'm sure it doesn't happen often." She felt herself melting—sensing the pain behind his pretense of arrogance, remembering the times during the night when he'd let himself be vulnerable to her. These moments with him would be engraved forever on her soul. But he was like a star that shone too brightly for her to stay around too long. Pete was more ordinary, less brilliant. Just like her. And that's what she had to go with. She sighed. She now had to be stronger than at any other time in her life. "I'm sorry, Dominic, for any way I've inconvenienced you."

He stood up and handed Gwyn the bag of beans. "It hasn't been an inconvenience, Gwyn." He walked to the door and put his hand on the knob. Her memory flashed back to his cabin, his hand on the knobs of his special cabinets, his hands on her. "I need to be going. Gwyn, I hope you find...whatever it is you hope to find." He looked her full in the eyes, then kissed her hand. "The Bound for Pleasure sails tomorrow at dawn." He turned on his heel and left.

Her eyes teared up as he walked out. She wished he'd turn around one last time, wave to her. He didn't.

"I'm glad he's gone," Pete muttered.

Gwyn couldn't say the same. But eventually, she was sure, the pain would fade. Maybe a decade or two...

"Come here," he said, putting the peas aside. "Give me a kiss."

She shook her head, then sat down cross-legged at his feet. "How are you feeling, Pete? Anything I can do?"

"He got me with a sucker punch," Pete looked down at his now frozen belly. "I'll be okay." Pete started to get up.

"Where you going?" she asked. After all, it was still fairly early Sunday, a day off for both of them.

"Gotta go home, change out of this costume. Big football game today with my buddies, and I can't show up in tights."

She couldn't believe he was just going to leave her like this. Not when she felt so hollow and bereft. She stood up.

"Don't go, Pete. Miss the football game so you can be with me and we can talk. After all, you just asked me to marry you." She was practically pleading with him. "We just started opening up to each other about some of our deepest feelings."

He looked at her as if she'd sprouted a second head, then a third. "Come on, babe. You know that that talking stuff is not where I'm at. At some point, I am willing to give it a try, if that's what floats your boat. But not now, not when my head's someplace else."

She scowled wondering what it would take to really get through to him. "I'm not just talking about talk. I'm talking about being together. Pete, we both have really hurt each other. Now we're talking about moving this relationship forward. But that's not going to just happen without a lot of effort — on both our parts."

"Tell you what," he said. "We can be together, but later. We've got all the time in the world. For now, it's really important for me to go to the football game." He paused for a moment, then his eyes widened as if with new inspiration. "Why don't you call up one of your girlfriends and talk with her. Get warmed up for when you talk to me. Have lunch, my treat. Look, you can even shop for an engagement ring. If you find something you like, put it on your credit card. I'll pay you back."

Gwyn was clutching her throat, realizing at last how clueless he really was. She visualized a possible future with Pete, days shopping with the girls because Pete was with his buddies at a football game or a baseball game or championship bowling or... Or was she the one who was being clueless?

She looked at him, wondering who this man really was. "Don't you *want* to be with me?" she asked.

He appeared to soften. "Hey, wasn't I waiting for you on your lawn all night? I even brought my buddies. And didn't I spend the whole morning with you? You want, I'll see you tonight. Get some pizza, a video… Chick flick or other garbage of your choice. Whatever you want." He looked pointedly at his watch. "But I've gotta get going now." He started walking to the door.

An incipient headache began to pound behind her eyebrows. "Wait, Pete." He stopped and turned to her. "I have one question. Why on earth did you propose to me this morning? Why when you hadn't even mentioned engagement or any sort of commitment before?" She really didn't know what to expect in his response.

He shrugged. "Hey, baby, once I saw Dominic Laredo sniffing around, I realized you must be something special. He only goes with prime women. I figured if you're good enough for him, you're good enough for me. And now, as I said before, the better man has won." He blew her a kiss, then opened the door and stepped out. "I'll call you later."

"Pete," she called out.

He turned looking annoyed. "What now?"

"Don't bother."

"Don't bother?"

"Don't call me. We're finished."

He shook his head. "I know you don't mean that. I'll call you tonight."

The door closed with a bang, just like she'd closed the door on being with Dominic. "I really do mean it, Pete," Gwyn called out softly to the closed door.

She sat down and put her face in her hands. With every cell in her body, every nerve ending, every atom and molecule, she knew that she'd made the right decision with Pete—and that she'd made a huge mistake in letting Dominic go. A huge, life-destroying mistake. She let her tears flow.

* * * * *

Dominic drove back to the Bound for Pleasure in a purple haze. He'd left the yacht and his business meeting as soon as Ned called to tell him something was awry with their plans. He'd excused himself from Laura, the rep, inviting her to stay on the yacht, promising he'd reschedule and finish their business shortly. He'd passed Ned in the Jaguar on the road to Gwyn's.

When Dominic got back to the yacht, he punched a wall…hard. Harder than he'd punched that fool Payne. He knew he should have followed his instincts and gone with Gwyn this morning. Then everything would have been all arranged by now, complete, and she'd be with him.

Could he have been so wrong about her? How could she have chosen Peter Payne over him? She'd seemed so positive that morning.

Dominic went back to the cabin, reliving his time with her the night before. Her scent and the fragrances of hot, heavy sex rose from his bed, nearly making him dizzy with regret. Well, he was leaving in the morning. He'd just have to get over being wrong, and start looking for the woman of his dreams elsewhere.

But he'd been so sure…

\* \* \* \* \*

The hours of the day stretched empty before Gwyn. She didn't have any friends available to see that day, any shopping to do, any book she could get interested in reading. Heck, she hadn't even picked up a Sunday paper, and now she didn't have the energy. If she'd gone ahead with her plans with Dominic, she'd have been real busy, choosing the things she wanted to take, contacting everyone as to where she'd be and how to stay in touch with her.

Boy, had she blown it. Might as well rename herself Hurricane Gwyn. Or Typhoon Gwyn. Heck, she was probably a tornado. As she sat alone, contemplating the debris of her life, she wondered how she'd managed to mess up this badly in so short a time. She'd had a man who was bigger and better than her dreams, wanting her to go off with him. And now Dominic thought she'd settled for Pete. For about three seconds, she'd reveled in the glorious freedom of being on her own. Being on her own was a lot better than being in a bad relationship, but when she compared it to sailing away with Dominic...

Gwyn patrolled her living room like a leopard stuck in a parakeet's cage. Dominic had a hold on her. He fascinated her and dominated her thoughts and feelings like no man she'd ever known before or would know in the future.

Gwyn thought back to all Dominic had shown her and shared with her the night before. He'd used the word "trust" with her. They'd both trusted each other, virtual strangers, with the various cuffs and ties. He'd wanted her to extend that trust in him to going away with him. She'd said yes, then abruptly reneged.

Could Dominic ever trust her again? He must hate her now. She couldn't blame him.

But could she make it up to him? It was Dominic she wanted, Dominic she should be with.

So what was holding her back? Pride? Yeah. Also fear. He might already have decided he never wanted to see her again.

After pacing for an hour, Gwyn realized there was no alternative. She would take the biggest risk of her life and go to him.

Maybe he'd reject her, the way she'd rejected him. She had to take that chance, put herself on the line. Playing it safe would cost her too high a price.

Once she'd made up her mind, Gwyn felt like she'd really sprouted Tinkerbell wings. She flew to her room, showered, and quickly threw on a winter white pants suit that always made her feel like Erin Brockovich. Not as sexy, just ballsy. Well, maybe sexy too.

Then she got in her old maroon Volvo and headed for the marina. While she drove, she mentally reviewed what she'd say to Dominic. She rehearsed her words, her attitude, then rejected each approach she came up with. She'd coolly announce she was going with him. She'd ask his forgiveness. She'd throw herself on his mercy.

By the time she arrived at the marina, Gwyn was talking to herself very loudly. She parked her car and finally told herself to shut up.

Even without the benefit of the glamorous lights and the starlit night, the Bound for Pleasure was a gorgeous craft. Gwyn stood before it for a moment, nearly awestruck. What the hell was she doing here? She had to be *nuts* to come here looking for Dominic. She could still turn around and go back home.

Not. Legs trembling, she began to climb the gangplank. There was no one on the deck when she stepped off. Maybe Dominic wasn't even there. She walked around, wondering where all the people were.

A tall redhead wearing the sexiest power suit Gwyn had ever seen came out to the deck sipping a margarita. She looked Gwyn up and down, then toasted her. "You here for a business appointment with the man too?" she asked.

"Business?" Gwyn asked.

The woman giggled. Probably not her first margarita. "That's what they call it." She leaned closer to Gwyn, as if to confide in her. "He may be a hot businessman, but it's nothing to what a hottie he is as a man."

Gwyn looked at her. Dominic a hottie? Big time. Had he found a woman to replace her with already? Gwyn had at least known Pete before she met Dominic. Maybe Dominic had known this woman before too. Maybe Gwyn should just turn around and go home the way she'd come.

The woman continued. "Had an appointment with him this morning. He got a phone call and rushed off in the middle like a volcano had exploded under him. Since he's been back, he's been too distracted to see me. Invited me to enjoy the bar. So I am. Wish he'd invite me to enjoy his bedroom. I've struck out big time on that. So far."

Could the redhead be talking about when Dominic had come to her house? Gwyn took a deep breath. Just then, Dominic appeared. He saw her and scowled, then turned to the other woman. "Laura," he said, "I apologize for keeping you waiting. This is not the way I usually conduct business. Please wait in my office—I'll be with you shortly." Laura swayed off.

"So I see you've found your way back to my yacht," Dominic said, not touching her. "Without Payne. What can I do for you? Maybe you want to borrow antique handcuffs or…"

Gwyn wished he would take her in his arms. "I'm so sorry," she said softly, looking him straight in the eye. "Dominic, I rejected Pete's proposal. And I've told him to leave me alone."

Dominic nodded. "Sounds like a good decision. Why did you need to come out to the yacht to tell me?"

He wasn't going to make this easy for her. She couldn't blame him. "It's not just Pete." She took a deep breath, preparing herself to say the most important words of her life. "Dominic, I know I made a mistake when I went back on my decision about coming with you. A huge one. Please, take me with you. But first, please take me in your arms."

He kept his face neutral and crossed his arms in front of him. "As you can see, I'm busy. Laura's been waiting all day to transact some simple business."

Well, he hadn't laughed in her face or thrown her off the yacht. Maybe there was still a glimmer of hope… "I'll wait for you so we can talk some more," she said, suddenly feeling the enormity of what she'd done.

He shrugged. "If you want to wait in the bar, suit yourself. I'm not sure how long I'll be."

He strode off. Gwyn went to the bar and got a diet soda. She drank a second and was contemplating a third when Dominic finally sat down opposite her with a glass of red wine.

"All finished with your business?" she asked, hoping to sound nonchalant.

"Is that what you waited here to talk about?" He took a sip of his wine.

"No, of course not," she said. She clenched her fists in her lap to keep from drumming her fingers on the table.

"Well, what is it?" He put down his wine glass and looked her deep in the eyes.

Now or never time, she told herself. She took a deep breath and plunged ahead. "Just this. I want to come with you."

He drew his brows together. "What's changed in the last few hours?"

She exhaled. "That's complicated to answer."

"I'm not leaving 'til morning."

Gwyn winced. "To make a very long story short, I realize that I didn't trust *myself* enough to go with you. But I do now."

Dominic sat stock still, looking at her intently. Surely he had to see the clear resolve in her face. Gwyn was sure she knew the moment he began to believe her, because his eyes went from the color of storm clouds to soft gray velvet. Then he smiled, stood up, and held out his arms for her. She rose to him and stepped into his warm embrace. Locked in his arms, Gwyn could feel the beating of Dominic's heart, hammering in time with hers. "Gwyn," he said at last, "are you really positive?"

She drew back for just a moment. "Yes," she said. "I was positive before. But I was too scared to pay attention."

"Now you're not so scared?"

## Hook, Wine & Tinker

"I'm not," she said. "Maybe a little, but I'm not going to pay attention to the part of me that's scared."

He looked at her with great tenderness. "Gwyn, you've got to learn to pay attention to all the parts — including the ones that are scared."

"That's hard to do."

He rubbed his hands down her back. "I know. But I'll be with you, if you want. We'll be together to look at your scared parts. And mine."

"You don't have any," she said.

"You'd be surprised," he answered. Then he took a deep breath. "Let's get practical. Do you want me to send a truck or van to the cottage to pick up your things?"

"No," she said. "Everything can wait. It'll get done. But not today."

"I like the way you think," he said, nodding.

"Think?" she echoed. She thought with her clit, which right now was throbbing for him. Hand in hand, they flew to Dominic's cabin. Once inside, he took her in his arms and kissed her, a deep thrusting with his tongue that left her gasping.

When her breath had returned, she asked, "So who are we going to make love as this time?"

Dominic furrowed his brow. "How about those great lovers, Gwyn Verde and Dominic Laredo?"

"Have I heard of them?" she asked.

"If you haven't before, you're going to now," he growled.

"Get out of those clothes," she growled right back.

"Yes, ma'am," he saluted. "You have to do the same."

She got totally naked, but he didn't. When he'd stripped down to his white silk boxers, she put her hands under the waistband and started to take them off him. "Those stay a bit longer," he said. She put her arms around his neck and pressed her breasts against him, sure he'd strip down in no time. "Not so fast," he said. "You want to have your way with me, but first things first."

She took a step back from him. "What do you mean?" she asked, both fearing and dying of curiosity.

Dominic looked at her sternly. "You've been a very bad girl, Gwyn."

"Well, yeah. And so?"

"Do you know what happens to bad girls?"

"They get big Hollywood contracts?"

He considered. "Extremely possible. But first they must be punished."

A delicious frisson shimmied up and down her spine. "Punished?" she asked. "What do you mean?"

He scowled. "You know I'm from England. We have a tradition in our schools of treating miscreants in a specific way. We spank them."

"Spank them?" she asked, her voice cracking. "You're going to *spank* me?"

"You'd better believe it." He sat down at the edge of his bed and signaled her to lie down across his long legs.

She positioned her belly right over his erection and applied appropriate friction. She felt his legs and balls tighten. Good.

He began to caress her butt. If this was his idea of a spanking... Suddenly he whacked her right cheek. Not very hard. She stifled a moan. She didn't want him to know yet how good that felt. After all, it was supposed to be a punishment.

Next he spanked the left cheek, a little harder. She felt a gentle sting, but also a whole lot of blood circulating to that spot in her anatomy. She pressed herself more firmly against his erection. He was one delicious man. "Oh, big master Dominic, you're punishing me so hard. I promise I'll be good. On second thought," she said when a third smack landed, "maybe I'm better off being really bad."

He started to laugh so hard that he couldn't land another spank. Gwyn ground her mound into him. If she maneuvered just right, she could probably get his cock in her...

He gave up with the spanking. "You're an impossible minx," he declared.

"Lose the boxers," she said, lying on his bed and opening her legs so he got a full view.

"Oh, Gwyn," he said, now naked, wriggling on top of her. "I couldn't stand it when I thought I'd lost you."

"Shh," she said, "we'll talk later."

"Right." He kissed her and they both entwined arms and legs, rolling around the bed. Both in too much of a rush for much more foreplay, they separated only long enough for her to stroke a condom onto his shaft. He lay down on his back and pulled her down on top of him. She sank down on his erection, surrounding him with her heat. She heard his sharp intake of breath.

"Gwyn," he said. "Oh, Gwyn."

She lay down on him, moving as slowly as she could, letting his cock come into contact with her smooth slick surfaces. She was so wet, she was afraid he'd slide out from under her. She clenched her thighs around him so he'd stay just where she wanted him.

She raised her hips, bringing her core almost to the tip of his penis. He put his hands on her lightly smarting ass and pulled her closer. She pushed tight against him and he thrust up into her, getting higher than ever before.

She rotated her hips, and he supported her with his hands. Oh, yes. Right there. She bit her lips to delay her release, with little effect. She was climbing up that mountain into the stratosphere, and nothing on God's green earth or in the heavens or the seas was going to stop her. She flew off the mountain and floated among the stars in deepest outer space. From somewhere far away she heard herself call his name. He was right there with her, orbiting the Earth, Jupiter, and Mars.

Replete, they lay in each other's arms. "Thank you, Dominic," she said.

"For what?"

"For giving me a second chance," she said, the moment too important for banter.

"I guess I won't make you walk the plank," he said.

He didn't.

At dawn, after a night filled with loving, they both lay entwined in deepest intimacy as the Bound for Pleasure weighed anchor and sailed away.

*The End*

# Pantasia 2:

# FOR PETE'S SAKE

Mardi Ballou

Preview

# Chapter One

"Be finished soon?" the custodian asked, turning on his vacuum cleaner. Pete Payne, startled by the machine's drone suddenly breaking the room's silence, looked up bleary-eyed at the man. They were the only ones still working at this hour of the night at the San Diego office of Fantasia Resorts, Inc.

"Just about done," Pete said, more to himself than the custodian, glancing at his Mickey Mouse watch and registering how really late it was. "Give me a minute, and I'll get out of your way." The man grunted and continued vacuuming.

Pete keyed in the final strokes to complete his project, logged off his computer, and cleared his desk with a satisfied sigh. Revenge, after all, was sweet. It was now late Tuesday night, Pacific time. By this time tomorrow, he'd be in Miami, en route to the Isla del Oro in the Caribbean. And on this coming Saturday, he'd watch the results of his scheme as an uninvited guest at the wedding of Gwyn Verde, his former almost-fiancée, and Dominic Laredo, the billionaire playboy, his soon-to-be-ex-boss. At the moment, Pete was the only person in the universe who knew the wedding was about to turn from an A-list social event to a black eye for Laredo.

Pete drove to a buddy's garage, where he'd stow his car while he was away. His friend, one of the "Lost Boys" he hung out with, would drive him to the airport in the morning. Still keyed up, Pete walked the mile and a half home from his friend's house. The quiet of the dark streets did little to calm him. He scrounged in his kitchen, munched the few remaining chips in the solitary bag lurking on top of the empty fridge, then hopped into the shower for a quick clean-up. As he dragged the comb through his too-long brown hair, he wondered if he should have gotten a haircut. His blue eyes red-rimmed with fatigue, he knew he had to get some decent sleep before he'd next see Gwyn.

After packing his duffel bag and laptop for the plane, Pete tried to settle down for the night. But sleep eluded him. As he began to think about seeing Gwyn in less than three days, Pete's smoldering resentment gave way to a tightening in his groin. He and Gwyn had been so good together. Without her in his life, he was experiencing new and unwelcome levels of horniness. Pete absentmindedly touched his burgeoning erection and closed his eyes.

There'd been no woman in his life since Gwyn had taken off with Dominic Laredo last fall. Here it was spring, when a young man's fancy and all that... And still no woman around except Griselda... Griselda, the semi-anatomically correct life-size inflatable doll his buddies had bought as a gag gift when Gwyn dumped him for Laredo. Some gag. These late nights, Griselda was beginning to look real good to him. Too good. He kept her sprawled on the chair next to his bed, on top of computer magazines, comic books, catalogs, and several Sunday sports pages.

Before Gwyn left him, it had been years since Pete had resorted to whacking off to relieve his tension. Now he spent so much time up close and personal with his right hand, he'd probably get the Gold Medal if jerking off ever became an Olympic event. Before Gwyn, he'd always found it easy to have girlfriends. Before Gwyn, he'd never let relationships become too complicated. Hell, he now realized he'd never really been involved in anything that could be called a relationship. Mutual satisfaction and uncomplicated good times—that's what he was all about. Pete winced, remembering Gwyn's complaints. Before she actually left, he'd always felt he had all the time in the world to make things right with her. She'd get over whatever bugged her. Instead, she got over him. His erection began to wilt—but by now, he was committed to going all the way with it. If he didn't come now, a middle of the night hard-on would sabotage any sleep he managed to get.

All he had to do was visualize Gwyn's luscious body spread out on his bed to get hard again. He didn't want to lose his momentum, so he increased the speed and intensity of his strokes. Jerking off was such a simple exercise—especially compared with the hard work of a relationship with a woman like Gwyn. But even now, as he pulled and prodded and stroked and stretched himself in all the right spots, he had to admit his hand came in a poor second.

At first, when Pete finally accepted that Gwyn was really gone, he wanted to resign from his job as a programmer for Laredo's Fantasia Resorts, Inc. But then he decided to bide his time. Because more than anything else, he wanted revenge on Dominic and a chance to win Gwyn back. So he continued to work at Fantasia, actually got accolades for his extra efforts, waiting for his shot at payback. And it came, faster then he'd ever anticipated.

Speaking of coming, Pete was really close to the edge. Imagining himself with Gwyn now, he squeezed harder and stroked faster—and then he thought about her upcoming wedding and lost the orgasmic spark. He groaned. Instead of the relief of a climax, he remained rock-hard and was starting to feel sore from all the frustrated friction.

Damn. Once Pete made Laredo look like a total fool in public, Gwyn would have to admit Pete was the better man after all. Pete couldn't get the vision of a supplicant, repentant Gwyn out of his mind. There she'd be, her gorgeous blonde hair sweeping over her face as she begged him to take her back.

Even that vision wasn't getting him off. Pete was about to reach for his *Victoria's Secret* catalog when Griselda, gleaming in the moonlight coming in the window, caught his eye. Griselda. Pete groaned, remembering the doll was semi-anatomically correct. He wasn't exactly sure what that meant, but it was beginning to sound amazingly...attractive.

Desperate, he reached over and pulled her into the bed, causing a mini-avalanche of the printed matter she'd been balanced on to spill onto the floor. Griselda's facial features included bright blue eyes and blood-red lips, wide open in a big *O* of surprise. Griselda, already obligingly nude, had large, albeit nippleless, breasts and a hairless triangle at the junction of her solid thighs. Pete ran his fingers over her bubble-gum pink plastic chest and his cock began to throb. If he squeezed her just right, Griselda expressed her one word vocabulary, which sounded like a cross between a groan and a fart. Music to his ears.

Pete lay down on his side and arranged Griselda to face him. "Come here often?" he asked, almost startled by the sound of his own voice in the darkness. When Griselda didn't answer, he squeezed her and interpreted her squeal to be a *yes*. He squeezed her several more times, and her syllable began to even more convincingly resemble a *yes*. He gently opened her legs and, with her *yesses* ringing in his ears, ran his cock along her mound. Alas, though her anatomy did include a hole there, its rough edges snagged at him like thorns from an aggressive rose. But her cool plastic exterior refreshed and excited his overheated penis, so he began to move his hips and hers to create a satisfying friction. Unfortunately, every time Pete thrust hard, Griselda's legs flew open, breaking their contact.

After several moments with Griselda's arms and legs flailing around and her limited conversation now more closely reminding him of excess gas than anything else, Pete's frustration began to rise almost as high as his erection. He grabbed her, hard, and turned her over. Pete discovered that Griselda's cheeks were more welcoming than her pussy triangle. Her maker must have been a butt man. Her buns were tight and full, and the crevice between them deep. Quick investigation by his fingers revealed a small smooth hole. That and the crack between her buns had Pete twitching with the expectation of relief.

He positioned Griselda on her stomach and lay down on top of her, which had her farting loudly in either protest or delight. After several moments of manipulation and experimentation, Pete found the perfect angle for approach. "Here I come, Griselda," he announced. This time when he thrust, Griselda stayed put. Well, hell, a little movement on her part would be welcome. Of course, Griselda being Griselda, Pete had to move her as well as himself. Which was okay. Within moments, Pete had fallen into a rhythm that had him tingling in anticipation. He'd never actually butt-fucked any woman, but now he began to wonder how it would be. Of course not every woman would be as agreeable to doing it as Griselda, but maybe the next time he was with a real woman he'd...

Griselda gave off a huge fart of excitement and Pete felt himself tighten as his body finally geared up for release. At least with Griselda, he didn't have to worry about a condom or having to use the "L" word... If only he could bring her to life, a plastic female Pinocchio... Pete ejaculated into and all over Griselda's buns and sighed with relief. Then he pushed her aside. Oh yeah, things were much simpler with this doll than with a real woman. And for the moment, that had some appeal. But Pete knew dolls like Griselda had a limited future as playmates. If he thrust too hard or dug his nails into her, he'd probably puncture her and she'd fly the hell off, probably get stuck on his ceiling. He needed a woman. He again toyed with the thought that Gwyn would come back to him. She'd always complained he treated her as thoughtlessly... Maybe like a plastic doll... Had he?

Pete tissued the cum off himself and his partner. "Thanks, honey," he said to her, not quite able to bring himself to kiss her but grateful all the same. "Thanks, guys," he added, sending a message to his buddies. At last his eyelids fluttered and sleep began to claim him.

\* \* \* \* \*

In the executive cottage that was one the perks of her job, Lily Tiger, manager of Fantasia Resorts' Isla de Oro Caribbean resort, was pacing the length of her bedroom. On this glorious moonlit Tuesday night, the sounds of the sea lapping up on the nearby beach would have lulled most people into sweet dreams. But Lily Tiger had not gotten to where she was by being easily lulled. At twenty-nine, she was the youngest manager in Dominic Laredo's empire—a position she'd held for two years. And her current position would be just the beginning of her professional rise.

But now, less than a week until the most important event of her career, Lily couldn't shake the gnawing dread that some catastrophe was brewing. Why did Dominic Laredo, her boss, have to choose the Isla del Oro for his wedding? Of all his resort sites—and all the other glorious resorts in the world that would love to accommodate him—why had he had to pick hers? She alternated between relishing the chance to shine and wondering what disaster lurked just over the horizon. Previously, she'd been confident she could handle anything that might come up. Now for the first time in years, she felt the chill breath of doubt and insecurity blowing an unwelcome breeze. She had to get back to her usual mindset pronto.

After all, Lily knew having Dominic Laredo at the Isla del Oro for his big day was a feather in her cap. When he'd announced his plans, the managers of all the other Fantasia resorts sent congratulatory emails—tinged green with jealousy. But her gut kept telling her to watch out. Her career path had been far too smooth—even though she'd worked her tush off for every advance and promotion. Now she had the greatest opportunity to move up to the big time in Dominic Laredo's organization—or to make a monumental ass of herself. Though she nearly rivaled her boss in her attention to the most minute of details, she kept thinking there was something she was just plain overlooking.

If she weren't keeping herself on a twenty-four/seven alert, she'd pour some chilled white wine to calm her nerves. Oh hell, she knew what she really needed—the right man to take her in his arms and love away her doubts. At this point, maybe she didn't even need him to be the *right* man in any of the usual meanings of that word—as long as he was right to cure what ailed her now.

Lily grinned to herself as her Cherokee grandmother came to mind. Old Alma had been cool, especially when she'd taught Lily about the care, feeding, and uses of men. Lily wished she could phone Alma right now, just to hear her calming words. But Alma was on her honeymoon in Hawaii with her fourth husband—and inaccessible for all but the most urgent of reasons. Horniness and nerves didn't qualify. Thoughts of her grandmother's recent marriage to a man twenty years her junior gave Lily a chuckle. Alma, having outlived her first three husbands, had chosen this time to wed one with some staying power.

Her grandmother had a more impressive track record than Lily when it came to men. In her career-building, Lily had relegated relationships to second level priority, just like the other major influence on her life, Aunt Dolores. By age thirty Dolores was CEO of a large food manufacturing conglomerate. Now in her fifties, Dolores was wealthy, successful—but profoundly alone. Lily absolutely believed that she could learn from both Alma and Dolores and have it all—the career and the love.

But right now Lily seemed to be following in Dolores's lonely footsteps. Lily's memories of her last…involvement, for want of a better word…made her frown. Though she hadn't expected commitment from Bert Stone, she'd demanded exclusivity. When she'd come back to her office after a business meeting to find him screwing her assistant on Lily's desk... Not only was that the end of Bert, but she'd also had to get a new assistant and a new desk. And Lily had been fond of both.

Damn, she missed him right now. Bert had known how to take her mind off business when she needed a break. There'd been no one since Bert, more than six months earlier. She wanted a superb lover who treated her with, in the words of the immortal Aretha, R-E-S-P-E-C-T. And TLC. Because at this moment, Lily's responsibilities and her horniness were rubbing her nerve endings raw.

But she had to get her mind off those nerve endings and that horniness so she could focus fully on Dominic Laredo's wedding. She'd reviewed all the plans seventeen hundred and fifty-six times. To give herself a shot at getting some sleep tonight, she'd review those plans for the seventeen hundred and fifty-seventh time. And maybe later she'd try out the brand new vibrator that had arrived in the day's mail.

So she read the wedding timetable and details over, checking off everything that was complete, noting what still needed attention. She looked up for a moment as starlight glinting in through the window reflected off Winnie, her bedroom desk owl. Lily liked to keep her huge collection of owls around her at home and at work. Her wisdom and love of order must have come from her owl nature. Which was often at war with her tiger nature, the only bequest she had from her long-gone father, Alfredo Tiger. She blamed him for the impatient masculine energy that had her twitching to call it a night. Owl won, and she settled in to work some more.

By two a.m. Wednesday, Lily had done everything she could. She yawned, stretched, and let her gaze wander over to her new vibrator. She picked it up, closed her eyes, and turned it on. It turned her on with its rhythmic vibrations in the palm of her hand. She turned it off and brought it with her when she crawled into bed. Tonight she enjoyed the feel of her smooth, cool, white-on-white silk sheets against her tired, overheated muscles.

Still tightly wound, Lily got the vibrator off her night table, pressed the button, and listened as it buzzed its song. Lily fingered her already moist, too long neglected pussy, then began to massage with her brand new toy. Her soft pink folds grew slicker, more than ready to accommodate her plastic friend. Despite her fatigue, Lily gave herself up to the mounting sensations emanating from her hungry core. As she massaged herself, she felt some of her long-held tension begin to dissipate. While she relaxed from her work problems, a different, more delicious tension took over. She tightened her legs and began to move faster as the longed-for orgasm began to grow. Lily loved the freedom she got from the isolation of her cottage. She could bounce on her bedsprings and sigh and gasp and make all the noise she ever wanted without concern for anyone hearing. Too bad there was no guy here making noises with her. Still, tonight she took advantage of her solitude to pant out her frustration and need, her release, as the vibrator took her up and over the crest of a short but very delicious come. Lily sighed, put aside the plastic toy, and closed her eyes.

And suddenly opened them as the details of the upcoming wedding reasserted themselves. The Parisian head chef and the Hollywood florist were scheduled to arrive first thing Thursday morning on Dominic's private jet. Several hours afterward, a chartered cargo jet would arrive from New York with the special foods and flowers Dominic had personally ordered. The chef and the florist would oversee the unloading and all the handling of the imported foods and flowers. If all went as it should, Lily wouldn't have much face-to-face time working with the chef and florist before the goods arrived. But she'd worked hard to set up communication lines among all the people who'd be working together to make the wedding happen. She'd had quite a job convincing the resident chefs and florists to share their turf with Dominic's imported honchos. But so far she'd managed to massage everyone's ego.

A small army of workers would also be arriving on Thursday, along with many of the three hundred wedding guests, and, oh yeah, Dominic Laredo and Gwyn Verde. Lily had managed to arrange reasonable accommodations for everyone, no small feat, but she still needed to check on a few last minute details that had arisen.

By the time she finished reviewing all the arrangements yet again, Lily's stress was back full force. There was no way she could function the next day without sleep. She reached to her bedside table again for her new purple companion, which she'd named Vincenzo. Vincenzo would put her to sleep. Vincenzo knew all the places that needed touching, rubbing. Within moments, Vincenzo was slick from Lily's orgasm. She put Vincenzo away and sighed. She needed to find a man soon. Or else buy more batteries...

Lily picked up Sophia, the little Italian marble owl she kept on her night table. Though she loved every owl in her collection, Sophia and Blanca, the plush white snow owl she kept between her pillows, were her favorites. When she got through Dominic's wedding, she'd treat herself to another owl—maybe two. And a vacation. A short one. Well, maybe not a vacation, not even a short one. But at least one new owl. She picked up the white snow owl and cuddled it to her as she fell asleep.

* * * * *

Once the plane bound for Miami was airborne, Pete booted up his laptop, plugged in to the air phone system, and dialed up his home office. Someone might catch his scheme in time to undo it. After several clicks on the keyboard, he saw that all systems were go. At the appointed hour, all Laredo's special orders would be consigned to an obscure Never Never Land. He disconnected and put his laptop to sleep, then wished he could do the same for himself. He sat back as far as possible in his tiny coach seat and stretched his long legs out, having to pull them back from the aisle every time someone went by. Forget sleep. He hated being scrunched up in the tiny "economy" seats. Gwyn wasn't flying coach any more these days. With Laredo, she'd be going first class all the way—or by private jet. Well, she might be flying first class, but their wedding would be not even third-rate.

Revenge was turning out to be easy. Laredo insisted on importing masses of food and flowers for the wedding. Of course. Pete volunteered to his supervisor, who wasn't aware of Pete's connection to Gwyn, to arrange for the delivery. Then Pete made just one *tiny* error in the itinerary for Laredo's jet. Pete simply keyed in an 's' instead of an 'r', a typo which could happen to anyone. Thus he'd routed several hundred thousand dollars' worth of gourmet foods and fancy flowers to the Isla del *Oso*, not the Isla del *Oro*. Instead of going to the Caribbean, all

Laredo's expensive, perishable cargo would end up on a remote island off the coast of Chile.

Pete patted himself on the back. The sheer simplicity of his scheme only enhanced its brilliance. By the time anyone would discover the mix-up, it would be far too late to correct. Aside from the distance between the two islands, the goods, including such delicacies as fifty-dollar-a-pound beef from Scotland, were far too spoilable to survive their being dumped in primitive storage facilities. So Dominic Laredo's wedding would be a piss-poor party with an inadequate supply of food and flowers. Laredo would be exposed, very publicly and very definitively, for the loser he was.

It would serve Laredo right to feel like a loser, for once. The way Pete had been feeling for months.

Pete's groin tightened at the thought of Gwyn begging to come back to him. He frowned a bit. Okay, so he hadn't worked this part out perfectly. Gwyn was pretty mad when she dumped him, and often before that. So maybe Pete would have to prove to her that he'd changed. That he'd learned what she wanted him to, though he wasn't exactly sure what that was. But Pete would work that out. He'd have to if he intended her to stay with him once she came back. He shifted in his seat. Once he had her with him again, he knew he could somehow be more responsive to her needs so that she'd never again want to leave.

The plane touched down just as the last rays of daylight faded. After getting his bearings in the noisy airport, Pete caught a shuttle to his motel. He took about three minutes to settle into his nondescript motel room, then dialed out for another check on the laptop. Everything was going fine.

Pete was not used to having a free evening. Tonight he couldn't even just hang with the Lost Boys—or Griselda. The long hours of the night stretched before him. He channel-surfed and found he had his choice between news, weather info, stale sitcoms, and old movies. What did people do for fun around here? If he stayed in his room, he'd probably be climbing the walls by ten o'clock Miami time—seven on his internal clock.

According to the TV listings, championship mud wrestling wouldn't come on for another two hours. Nothing else snagged him. So Pete took himself down to the bar off the motel lobby. He'd treat himself to a brew and get some dinner.

At the bar's entrance, pink plastic flamingos—possibly Griselda's avian cousins—cavorted under swaying palms on a paper mural. Three guys, tired business travelers trying to sell the wrong products, sat on stools, drank beer, munched peanuts, and exchanged occasional small talk. The bartender, a redhead who looked like she'd been around the block one too many times, frowned as she mixed a drink while two TV pundits blared out their dissection of the afternoon's ball game. Pete sat at the end of the bar farthest away from the businessmen and ordered a Dos Equis.

"Where 'ya from?" the bartender, whose nametag identified her as Nan, asked.

"San Diego," Pete grunted.

"Pretty city," she said. When she smiled, Nan looked a bit less haggard. "So why's a California guy coming to Miami? Can't be pleasure, so it must be business, right?"

"Right," Pete said, raising his glass in mock salute.

Nan glanced down the bar at the other customers. No one else appeared to need her immediate services. "Are you buying or selling here in Miami?"

Pete toyed with the idea of making up some response, then decided it wasn't worth the effort. "Neither. I'll be catching a plane to Puerto Rico in the morning." He downed a big swallow of his beer.

"Puerto Rico? What are you going to..."

He cut her off. "Hey, Nan. No business talk tonight, at least not about me. So, you been in Miami long?"

"Just since my old man split, three years now. We lived in Minnesota." She shook her head.

"Minnesota?" Pete chuckled. "That's quite a change."

Nan shrugged. "I had more than enough cold gray winters to last me two lifetimes. And I can see all the snow I want in photos. I look at them, and when I get tired, I shut the book." Nan wiped the already spotless counter with a cloth.

Pete took another sip of his beer and studied her. "So why Miami instead of, say, San Diego?"

She rubbed her fingers together indicating cash. "It's way cheaper to live here, otherwise I'd be out there in a shot. I always dreamed of living in California." Her eyes took on a faraway look, and she seemed almost pretty in an older woman way.

He nodded. One of the businessmen signaled Nan for a refill. Two more men and a woman entered the bar. The various conversations began to liven up the place. Pete watched Nan as she gracefully and efficiently went about her job. He was surprised to realize he found her company a reasonable distraction from his restlessness.

When she'd served everyone, Nan looked over at Pete who nodded that yes, he'd like a refill. He smiled, signaling he'd also enjoy her company. Actually, at this point he preferred her company to the beer. Pete dipped into the basket of nuts and pretzels Nan had left earlier. His stomach rumbled, and Pete became aware that he was hungry for more than bar munchies. He'd just swallowed his second handful when Nan brought his beer, which he left untouched.

"So what time do you get off tonight?" Pete asked, surprising himself with his question.

Nan appeared equally surprised—and pleased. She looked at her watch. "The other bartender comes on in half an hour. It being so quiet here tonight, I could probably leave in an hour or so, after she gets settled." Nan blushed, which Pete found charming.

"Would you come out with me for some dinner? I hate to eat alone."

A flicker of what almost looked like disappointment passed over her face. "I could fix you a sandwich here at the bar or get you a burger and fries from the grill."

Pete's stomach rumbled again, this time so loud Nan had to hear it. "A burger and fries sounds great," he said. Seeing her look expectantly at him, he added, "I'd still like you to leave with me when you can." He'd have liked to eat with her, but he was too hungry to postpone his meal any longer.

Nan lowered her lashes and smiled. "You've got it. Now let me get that order in for you. They'll send it over right away. How do you like your burger?"

"Medium, ketchup, and onions. Lots of fries. You have those curly ones?"

"Just the long kind."

"That'll do."

Nan spoke the order into an intercom, then waited on some other customers. Pete watched her bend over, revealing excellent legs as her short pink uniform skirt rode up to within inches of tight round buns. Pete shifted as he felt his groin tighten. He'd never been with an older woman, not in any way. But something about Nan appealed to him. Her being clearly so much older almost added an air of exoticism, as if her age were some foreign country or unusual ethnicity.

She soon brought him a plate with a huge burger and an impressive order of fries. As he was still nursing his third beer, Pete said he didn't want anything else to drink. He saw Nan watching him while he ate. The burger tasted unusually delicious, as if he hadn't eaten for days. Was it Nan's eyes on him that heightened its flavor? As the meat's juices flowed into him, Pete felt a reawakening of his senses — which had been hibernating since when? Since Gwyn had left him? Had it really been so long since anything had tasted — or looked — so good to him?

The fries stood up to the burger in quality. Crispy on the outside, soft inside, salted and herbed to perfection. He held out his plate to Nan, offering her a fry. "Not when I'm on duty," she said, her voice low and sultry.

Pete savored his impromptu meal, relishing every morsel of the food, feeling satisfied when he'd gobbled the final fry and sipped the last of his beer. Nan's counterpart, a young graduate student named Maya, arrived early and was more than willing for Nan to leave before the official end of her shift.

"Thanks, darlin'. I owe you one," Nan said to Maya.

Maya waved dismissively. "Have a great time. See you tomorrow."

"Give me just a minute to change," Nan said to Pete, walking into a room marked Employees Only. True to her word, she stepped out moments later having changed from her pink uniform to black slacks and a white pullover.

Now Pete realized he didn't know where to take Nan. He couldn't just ask her up to his room... "Where can we go to be alone and talk?"

"I know a little club where we could listen to some music," she said, giving her hair a pat and taking his arm to walk out.

"Sounds great. Uh, how do we get there?"

She smiled at him. "In my car," she said, leading him over to an ancient lime green VW Bug with daisies painted on its doors.

Pete climbed in and got comfortable in the little car. Nan drove with assurance, getting them to a strip mall in ten minutes. Pete was relieved to find that, just as advertised, Nan was taking him to a small place, just a few tables and a simple bar. Tonight a pianist played jazz improvisations softly in the background.

"I've had enough of being at a bar for tonight," Nan said. A hostess led them to a table for two in the corner farthest from the piano. A server came over to get their orders. Though he wasn't going to drink much more, Pete got another beer, Nan a margarita.

"Thanks for coming out with me," Pete said.

Nan looked him in the eyes. "How old are you, Pete?"

He scowled. "Why?"

She laughed dryly. "I don't even know your last name or what kind of work you do. Look at me asking your age first." She shrugged. "Just one of my Midwest hang-ups, I guess."

Pete found Nan more and more appealing with each word she said. "Payne. P-A-Y-N-E. A computer geek. Still want to know how old I am?" he asked, reaching out to take her hand in his.

"Yes," she said softly.

"I'm thirty. How much does it matter?"

"Sullivan. A potter and a bartender. Fifty-two. How much does it matter to you?"

Pete grinned easily. "Not at all." He found he actually meant what he said. He traced the lines in her left palm with his index finger. "Nan Sullivan, I'm glad I met you."

The server's arrival with their drinks briefly intruded on the growing warmth between them. Pete found it both soothing and exciting to have Nan with him—and time off from his obsession with Gwyn. "To older women," he said, raising his beer stein in salute.

"And younger men." She clinked her margarita glass against his stein.

They both chuckled and drank, Nan deeply, Pete very little.

"So you're heading off to Puerto Rico in the morning," Nan said. "Will you be coming back this way when your business is done?"

Pete shook his head. "No such plans...at this time. Except to pass through again."

She nodded and took another sip of her drink. "So, how long will it take you to finish what you're doing in Puerto Rico?"

The last thing Pete wanted to talk or think about now was the Isla del Oro project, as he'd labeled it in his head. How could he steer the conversation elsewhere than Nan's perfectly reasonable questions? Gwyn's complaints that he rarely asked about her suddenly popped into his mind. And Pete was vaguely aware that women liked to talk about themselves. Hell, women liked to talk, period. Well, might as well give that a try. So he shook his head again. "Don't want to talk about that. Would much rather hear about you, Nan."

She shrugged. "Familiar story. Was married for twenty-five years to my high school sweetheart. Our wedding was the day after I graduated. He was a year ahead of me. We had four kids together—and now two grandchildren with a third on the way. It all ended three years ago. Jerry, that was my husband, had the typical mid-life crisis. Found his way through it by climbing into the sack with his twenty-three year old secretary." She began shredding a cocktail napkin. "They're now the proud parents of twin boys." She laughed dryly. "Jerry's doing diaper duty. His wife must be quite a woman if she gets him to do that." She tore the last of the napkin, then pushed the debris into a small pile alongside her drink.

Pete was finding he actually liked the process of getting to know this woman, and not just so he could get her in the sack. "Obviously a man of limited intelligence and taste."

Nan smiled. "I like to think so. My oldest daughter moved down here to Miami four years ago. She invited me to her house for some R and R after Jerry... When I'd wept my last tear, I decided to move here to be with her and her family and start living *la vida loca*. Though I'll tell you, if I had the bucks, I'd have gone to San Diego. But here I am." Her voice trailed off.

"You said you're a potter as well as a bartender?"

Nan grinned broadly. "A hobby I want to turn into a business. I used to make dishes, vases, that sort of thing, at the Y. Always gave them to friends and family for Christmas. I figured everyone was just humoring me when they acted happy to get my stuff." She blushed. "Imagine my surprise when people began asking me to make different pieces for them. I never thought a person could turn something they love doing into a business. I'm in the process of learning how to do that."

"I bet you'll be great," he said, and meant it. "So where does that bartending fit in?"

"I call it my day job at night. Helps pay the bills 'til the pottery catches on."

"My money's on you. I bet you hit it big soon."

"From your mouth to God's ear," Nan said, toasting him again.

"Come back to my room with me, Nan Sullivan. Stay with me tonight."

Grinning, she stood up and flung her purse over her shoulder. "I thought you'd never ask."

## About the author:

Exploring the erotic side of romance keeps Mardi Ballou chained to her computer—and inspires some amazing research. Mardi's a Jersey girl, now living in Northern California with her hero husband—the love of her life—who's also her tech maven and first reader. Her days and nights are filled with books to read and write, chocolate, and the pursuit of romantic dreams. A Scorpio by birth and temperament, Mardi believes in living life with Passion, Intensity, and Lots of Laughs (this last from her moon in Sagittarius). Published in different genres under different names, Mardi is thrilled to be part of the Ellora's Cave Team Romantica.

Mardi Ballou welcomes mail from readers. You can write to her c/o Ellora's Cave Publishing at 1337 Commerce Drive, Suite 13, Stow OH 44224.

**Also by Mardi Ballou:**

Pantasia 2: For Pete's Sake (sequel to Hook, Wine & Tinker)
Photo Finish
Young Vampires in Love, Autumn 2004

# Why an electronic book?

We live in the Information Age—an exciting time in the history of human civilization in which technology rules supreme and continues to progress in leaps and bounds every minute of every hour of every day. For a multitude of reasons, more and more avid literary fans are opting to purchase e-books instead of paperbacks. The question to those not yet initiated to the world of electronic reading is simply: *why?*

1. *Price.* An electronic title at Ellora's Cave Publishing runs anywhere from 40-75% less than the cover price of the <u>exact same title</u> in paperback format. Why? Cold mathematics. It is less expensive to publish an e-book than it is to publish a paperback, so the savings are passed along to the consumer.
2. *Space.* Running out of room to house your paperback books? That is one worry you will never have with electronic novels. For a low one-time cost, you can purchase a handheld computer designed specifically for e-reading purposes. Many e-readers are larger than the average handheld, giving you plenty of screen room. Better yet, hundreds of titles can be stored within your new library—a single microchip. (Please note that Ellora's Cave does not endorse any specific brands. You can check our website at www.ellorascave.com for customer

recommendations we make available to new consumers.)

3. *Mobility.* Because your new library now consists of only a microchip, your entire cache of books can be taken with you wherever you go.

4. *Personal preferences are accounted for.* Are the words you are currently reading too small? Too large? Too…**ANNOYING**? Paperback books cannot be modified according to personal preferences, but e-books can.

5. *Innovation.* The way you read a book is not the only advancement the Information Age has gifted the literary community with. There is also the factor of what you can read. Ellora's Cave Publishing will be introducing a new line of interactive titles that are available in e-book format only.

6. *Instant gratification.* Is it the middle of the night and all the bookstores are closed? Are you tired of waiting days—sometimes weeks—for online and offline bookstores to ship the novels you bought? Ellora's Cave Publishing sells instantaneous downloads 24 hours a day, 7 days a week, 365 days a year. Our e-book delivery system is 100% automated, meaning your order is filled as soon as you pay for it.

Those are a few of the top reasons why electronic novels are displacing paperbacks for many an avid reader. As always, Ellora's Cave Publishing welcomes your questions and comments. We invite you to email us at service@ellorascave.com or write to us directly at: 1337 Commerce Drive, Suite 13, Stow OH 44224.